The
Sweet Birds
of Gorham

The Sweet Birds of Gorham

a novel

Ann Birstein

Distributed in 2015 by Open Road Distribution
345 Hudson Street
New York, NY 10014
www.openroadmedia.com

For my daughter

The Sweet Birds of Gorham

1

AS ALWAYS WHEN DAISY LERNER WAS WAITING for something very hard she was absent when it finally came. She had been staring out the window sipping coffee from a wet container and making up a story about a young man *in March of 18—traveling from Minsk to St. Petersburg,* when the conductor called "Gor-ham next! Gor-ham next!" and called it again three more times before Daisy realized he was talking to *her.* Whipping down her suitcase, she bopped the college boy who had been sitting beside her on the head with it, apologized, scurried frantically down the aisle to the wrong door, scurried back the other way, and was lifted off the train by the elbows just in time. With the first burst of energy it had shown all afternoon the Green Valley Local whooshed away from the platform, leaving Daisy with a sudden but unmistakable impression that she had just been exposed from the rear.

After a moment or two, she smoothed down her skirt. The hush around the station was fragrant and gravelly. Also, although the violently flickering lights of the train had convinced her it was raining outside, the day was surprisingly clean and bright. Setting down her suitcase between her ankles, Daisy took a deep breath of the fresh air as she had been taught to do whenever she found herself in the country. A breeze came rustling across the treetops and tickled her chin with her own thin white collar. She giggled a little and then immediately felt out of place, since the few other people on the platform continued to suffer the same mild forms of outrage that had afflicted them on the train, including the elderly lady from Boston who kept comparing her timetable with the watch pinned to her bosom and quivering in the jowls, and the three girls from Mount Holyoke who had been playing bridge the whole way up and now rubbed their toes on their ankles in an ecstasy of boredom. Even her former seat mate, the college boy with the long legs and acne, had stuck away the cowbell he had been clanging as he cried "Toonerville Trolley!" and was picking at his chin while he stared at her morosely. Daisy smiled, but rather more sadly than she had expected to at that moment. It made her feel terrible to be the only happy one when everybody else was unhappy and it was beginning to occur too frequently. She was always skipping along gaily, like a child at hopscotch, until somebody tapped her on the shoulder and reminded her that life was tragic. Is it because there's always room in my heart, Daisy wondered, and everybody else's seems to be booked solid? *Oh, Gorham*, she apostrophized cautiously, shooting another quick look behind her . . . *I'm here . . . I'm yours, in case you're interested*. . . . A fresh tickling breeze from across the street, but otherwise no dice. *Oh, life, fill me up?* Life obliged. The hot September sun slid from behind a tree and hit her full in the face. It was blinding and gorgeous.

The sun slid back again, leaving Daisy slightly out of breath, but considerably dappled. It had not dawned on her before how incredibly rural the landscape was. And all in picture-magazine colors of autumn. Murky blue hills in the distance. Against them clumps of the brightest yellow, the deepest green, a blot of crimson, a streak of rust. A white nest of houses, a neat red barn, a church steeple, a mottled cow, a bush of wildly flowering orange flowers. Across the cinder path, a willow or other weeping tree dipped its branches in pond water.

"Sweet Jesus," Daisy murmured, "I really *have* landed in the country."

"I'll bet *you're* from New York," the college boy said, bestirring himself with a faint interior clank.

"New York?" Daisy repeated reluctantly. "Well, yes, I suppose you might say I am."

"And never seen a tree before, huh?"

"I have seen trees," Daisy said, pointedly ignoring the loud guffaw. "I have simply never seen these particular trees."

"How come? Aren't you from Smith?"

"Gorham."

"Don't give me that," her companion said, with a wink that advised against putting anything over on him. "The Gorham girls don't come until Monday. *I* ought to know."

"But I'm not a student, you see," Daisy said, sweetly playing her trump at last. "I happen to be a teacher."

"Oh?" the boy said, "I thought you were younger."

It was on the tip of Daisy's tongue to tell him that she *was* younger, at the outside a year or two older than he—especially if he was as dumb as he looked, and if you took into consideration that Daisy had skipped three times in grammar school—until she belatedly remembered the new dignity of her position. No, there was no point in confiding in this buster. With him she was playing it close to the chest.

"Let's just say," Daisy said simply, "that I'm embarking on a new adventure."

"Yeah? Well, look me up some time," he said, snapping his fingers jazzily. "Maybe I can show you some more adventure. Maybe I can show you some more scenery. The name's Pete."

A painted and inscribed Model T Ford rolled up and she thoughtfully watched him leap into it and vanish in a fitting cloud of black exhaust. Perhaps if he had been an older man with sympathetic eyes, she might have told him that appearances to the contrary notwithstanding she was not only a teacher, but also an author. Of one short novel—or one long short story, to be painfully exact—which had been anthologized in a paperback of Young Moderns the year before only to sink without a trace into the murky depths of the Sunday *Times* where it was reviewed seven months too late. And that after straining her ears for the last gurgle . . . oh, well. Flipping open her compact, Daisy blinked at herself interestedly once or twice (her eyes were blue, the color of cornflowers she had been told, which somehow sounded bluer than cornflowers actually were), and poked at a couple of whitish blond curls near her temples. Yes, of course she had dreamed—who wouldn't?—of lying around in a checked weskit, of center spreads in *Mademoiselle*, of a reputation for not giving interviews. But if what she had told that loutish boy was true, why dwell on it now? Still, as she put the compact away again, Daisy could not help realizing that if she had been a character in one of her own works that quick oval glimpse would have revealed the whole of her to herself instantly—the unfortunate influence of Henry James and his central observer—whereas all *she* had seen was a fragment, a bit of colored Rorschach which might have developed into a head of Voltaire, or possibly Harpo Marx, or even a Yiddishe Shirley Temple, each of whom she had been compared to at one time or another. A terrible shame, really, when life failed to imitate art.

Bending to untwist a stocking heel, she waited a moment, half straightened-up—was anything profound happening to her yet emotionally? no—and then decided to ask directions of the Railway Expressman, who was staring at her anyway.

"69 Elm Street?" he repeated, fingering a rotund watch chain. "You figuring to walk?"

"You mean it's dangerous?" Daisy asked. "Or just too far?"

"How's that?"

"Actually," she confessed laughingly, "I almost never walk by myself. I'm always thinking that other people are thinking about me. And also I'm afraid of dogs."

"Yup. There's lots of dogs in Gorham."

"But today, you see, happens to be a special day in my life. I'm on my way to my first teaching job—my first *any* job, actually—and also my first apartment."

"Ayuh. Well, it's not too far unless you go by way of Crescent. But you wouldn't want to do that."

"No."

"Then you want Main. Let's see. . . ."

More meditative head scratchings followed by a series of complicated directions which Daisy thanked him for as she pondered her first lesson about Gorham: that apparently none of its citizens ever walked, which was strange since in Winesburg, Ohio, people were always strolling off and telling each other everything. Her first sight of Main Street, which turned out to be a few short blocks away, was even stranger. Could it be that she had spent a morning of oxbows and junctions only to wind up in one of the better parts of Queens? But no. Forest Hills was a mere acorn. The town of Gorham was an *oak*, so obviously certain it smelled sweet and clean down to the roots that the few middle-aged people strolling by looked relieved to have awakened here instead of someplace else. Or perhaps what gave them that particular air of satisfaction was knowing that they had been granted the best of two possible worlds simultaneously: such as the diner on one side of the street, and the Tudor mansion with a boar's head sign reading "Ye Gorham Inn" on the other; the modern drugstore with a Revlon display, succeeded in short order by an old-fashioned pharmacy with bottles of colored water and apothecary jars filled with rock candy and horehound drops in its window. For a few blocks more Main Street continued in this manner, alternating its supermarket with a branch of Lord and Taylor and a white church and steeple, the hardware store with an 1890 Town Hall, until suddenly it divided itself with a flourish to entertain a large grassy commons, so green and smooth and English that Daisy looked around for the villagers to come prancing across it and wind their colored ribbons around the parking meters. The commons was obviously Gorham's way of pointing with pride toward its college, for at the end of it, on a little hill of its own, stood a tall filigreed gate half strangled with ivy and bearing the legend "Gorham College for Females." Splendid. Tipping her mortar board, Daisy left its pleasures for later, turned right, and confounded herself by having arrived at Elm Street without any mishap at all.

Here she put down her suitcase, which was a present from her older sister Sylvia along with a lot of unwelcome comments about burying herself in a small college town— "Listen, *nobody* breaks up with a nice boy like Ronald because she *isn't* pregnant!"—and gave herself a rest, flexing and unflexing her hand. Something was nagging at her which had started at the station, and she could not figure out what it was. Homesickness? No, the big apartment, her mother's Italian-style silver-flecked hair already shone as distantly as the moon.

Money? Only when she began to wonder if her father, that amiable furrier, expected her to *live* on her salary. Sex? Unfortunately, she could still hear Sylvia, who was married to an accountant, begging her never to tell her own husband anything about the past because what a man didn't know wouldn't hurt him. Which, like all of Sylvia's handy hints was of questionable value—wouldn't it hurt a man more?—but had nevertheless lodged itself in Daisy's mind accreting other thoughts around it, like an irritant planted in an oyster shell. Sylvia had also been positive that Daisy was only inviting more trouble to live in an apartment all by herself. A typical Sylvia prophecy and unrelated to what was still bothering her, though it managed to brighten Daisy considerably. She trotted off again, leaving Sylvia still giving out advice, but to a departing audience.

Elm Street was beckoning to her. A truly noble avenue, bordered by tall trees (elms!) which entwined their branches overhead into a thick rustling canopy. Beneath it, the street was a dim mysterious aisle, carpeted with fallen leaves. Daisy bowed her head, and taking small solemn steps, a little lopsided and wobbly on account of the suitcase and high heels, prepared to enter this strange new kingdom. She assumed that Gorham was about to open its arms to her. She also assumed that until she had made herself known, there would not be a soul on Elm Street to tell who she was, much less care.

"Nice ass," Seymour Lipshansky remarked from his vantage point of instructor of English, and then with a shrug and a yawn let the edge of the curtain slip back through his fingers to blot out the fleeting though delectable sight at his window. He buried himself deeper in his bathrobe, like a turtle seeking the safety of its own shell. It was a nice bathrobe, a little soiled maybe—his wife had given it to him as an engagement present—but of the most durable English wool, which it needed to be considering the time Seymour spent in it.

"Whose ass?" his wife said, sitting beside him on the sofa and making out checks signed Julia Clark Lipshanksy.

"Oh, some girl who just walked by," Seymour said with an innocent smile.

"Which girl?"

"I don't know. Somebody from the college, I suppose," Seymour guessed, not with any great difficulty since the college owned all the houses on Elm Street. "Can't be a student, though. The dorms don't open until Wednesday. Oh, I know—it must be the new one Dudley got the apartment for and was talking about."

"Daisy Lerner," Julia said distinctly. "Tootsie Goldfarb is holding her key."

"Yeah, that one," Seymour said.

Giving him a quick sideways glance, Julia bent back over the check-book again, keeping a hand on the untidy pile of papers in her lap. Bills, bills, bills, Seymour thought, wearily flexing his long bare feet against the do-it-yourself coffee table, and squinting with a sudden, new-found interest at the do-it-yourself bookcases on the opposite wall. He put on his glasses. It had just occurred to him that almost all of his furniture had been done by himself and that for a man who was all thumbs he had spent an awful lot of his married life nailing and ham-mering, since in addition to the coffee table and the bookcases, he also seemed to have put together the dining-room table—a board mounted on a wrought iron stand—the hi-fi cabinet, still unvarnished, the also unvarnished chests of drawers for the five tiny bedrooms upstairs, the beds themselves—mattresses hauled on top of box springs into which he had screwed sets of legs—and also. . . . Seymour lacked the energy to go on. Besides, it was a point of pride never to be burdened by pos-sessions, in any sense of the phrase. Not that people didn't sometimes talk. They would make remarks about the large abandoned swing rot-ting away on the Lipshansky front porch, and the fact that the last spring thaw had uncovered a sled and a boot in the flower bed which were now waiting for the next snowfall to cover them up again, and also mutter exceedingly nasty things when they happened to trip over a toy truck or two on the living-room floor. But what difference did it make? It did not even actually bother Seymour that his home, as he had just realized, was practically a warehouse of splintering wood and raw fabrics. No, the only thing he owned that had ever actually stuck in his craw was the one piece of furniture, oddly enough, that had been finished off and polished in a factory—an enormous refrigerator sold to him at an unrefusable bargain rate by Edgar Dudley, professor in charge of basketball and housing, and the crookedest son of a bitch who had ever stalked the groves of Academe.

"You know, come to think of it," Seymour said casually, "we ought to have her over one of these days."

"Who?"

"You know, that kid. I mean what the hell, it's lonely around here at the beginning and the lower echelons ought to stick together."

Julia looked at him silently.

"I better get to work?" Seymour suggested, though he made no attempt to rise.

Still no peep out of Julia. In spite of himself, Seymour had to hand it to her. She could certainly be a perfect gem of nonexpression when she wanted to, the crystallization of many years of fine background and breeding, and sedate Philadelphia suburbs, and family subscriptions to chamber music series, and clothes selected from a Best and Co. catalogue. Yes, of course that was it, Seymour decided as Julia's look continued to pinion him and he remembered that as a literary historian he could clutch at larger issues: his wife was a product of a culture so homogeneous there was nothing she was required to do or say. As in the case of her motherhood, for example, which happened to be a large consideration since Julia had four lusty children and a reputation for being an excellent mother to them. (Even the children thought of her as an excellent mother to them.) But when Seymour looked for some evidence to support this general opinion, which he also shared, there didn't seem to be any. Did the lady sitting beside him with the family checkbook ever sing to her kids, for instance, or pinch their behinds, or give them a kiss when no kiss was indicated? Not at all. She had merely given birth to them, which in Julia's case was more than sufficient. And then there was Julia's entire physical set-up, Seymour meditated, warming up to his subject, who was unfortunately still keeping an eye on him. When he first met Julia on his way out of the army he would have sworn that she was tall and statuesque (could a Clark woman be anything else?). But lately it had begun to dawn on him that his wife was short and dumpy and, for a well-bred girl, very schmaltzy in the thigh. As the light spilling below the curtain was troubling to point out, there was more than a little gray in Julia's blond pageboy these days, more than one wrinkle in her pert baby face. But it did not matter. Julia was still essentially an undergraduate in one of the better women's colleges, Gorham itself in this case. What a life: to be without doing, to look without saying. All of which explained, at least to Seymour's satisfaction, why when Julia looked at a man silently there wasn't anything he could put his finger on. She wasn't accusing or condescending or condemning. She was only looking. You were the one who squirmed, or thought up alibis, or defended yourself heatedly or tried to change the subject. You were the one who. . . .

Outside it was suspiciously quiet. The four Lipshansky children had gone to play by the railroad tracks. One of these days one of them was sure to get killed. But as Julia always said mildly, if you kept them from roaming around they would feel smothered and overprotected. Still, it would be a relief when they all came trotting home safely again. Though when they did there would be so much noise and mess it would be impossible to get any work done. And no one, not even the head of his department, could blame a man for not being sufficiently productive when at thirty-seven he was already saddled with four demanding children, and a home, and a wife, and. . . .

"Oh, now look, Julia, don't be stupid," Seymour said, and involuntarily glanced back at the window.

"I *beg* your pardon. My name is Daisy Lerner, and I wonder if . . ."

Daisy's voice broke off. Amid the white empty porches the plump woman in the flowered housedress sat as if she were on a stoop between Essex and Delancey. She was fanning herself between the thighs with a taut piece of her skirt and also rocking a baby who dozed sweatily beside her in a canvas teeterbabe.

"It's okay, doll," Tootsie Goldfarb reassured her, smiling and squinting against the sunshine, "no need to aggravate. You came to the right place. Also—" she indicated her blossoming pocket with an elbow—"I have the key right here."

"Oh, I'm so glad," Daisy said, putting down her suitcase with a sigh of relief, "because sometimes when you confront a new situation everything gets balled up right away, do you know what I mean?"

"Not in Gorham," Tootsie disagreed cheerfully, "not in this town."

"And still," Daisy said, "I suppose you'll think this is ridiculous, but all the way up Elm Street under that incredible canopy of trees, I thought suppose she doesn't have the vaguest notion who I am, suppose Mr. Whatsis entirely neglected to—"

"*Dudley*," Tootsie said, checking a rock in mid-motion and giving her a quick warning smile like a dagger. "Dudley doesn't neglect anything. Also, doll, you should try to remember his name because, believe me, he'll never forget yours."

"Really?" Daisy laughed. "He sounds as if he owns a powerful chain of newspapers or something."

"In Gorham it's housing that makes or breaks you, darling, not Hearst," Tootsie said. "As a matter of fact," she added casually, "you just missed him by a few hours. He and my husband went hunting this morning."

"Your husband hunts?"

"Why not? It's a free country, isn't it? Why shouldn't Milton Goldfarb hunt?"

"No reason," Daisy said quickly. "And no offense meant, I assure you."

"Yeah," Tootsie assured her back after a moment, patting her enormous chignon ("I stuff it with a whole roll of cotton," she explained sheepishly), ". . . yeah, sure, no offense taken."

Beside her the baby made a mewing sound and Tootsie gave him a few extra rocks to keep him asleep.

"Yes," Daisy said. "—well, anyway, that's a nice fat baby you have there."

"I feed him up," Tootsie said.

"Oh, really?"

". . . but, listen, you're Jewish, right?"

"Oh, yes."

"But the hair. It's natural blond? Not even a permanent?"

"No. I mean yes."

"So okay, doll," Tootsie shrugged, producing the key at last along with a new bright, juicy smile, ". . . here. Take it. Enjoy yourself."

Thanking her profusely and wondering why the occasion demanded quite so much gratitude, Daisy clattered back down the walk, not realizing that she was humming "Toot-toot-tootsie good-bye" until at the end of Elm Street the song suddenly died on her lips. An enormous gray house confronted her. She pushed away the vine on the gatepost and found the number. 69, Daisy read, realizing that she was home at last. And, as the vine embraced the gatepost again, that in Gorham houses made a point of not advertising their addresses. (Out of pride, perhaps, because they were ashamed of no longer being called the Old Lacey Place or Mrs. Smith's Cottage?) But her heart had told her this was it and she had always made a point of trusting her heart implicitly even when, as now, this first sight of her new home had contracted it to the size of a baby's fist.

From the foot of the long grassy walk where she stood, suitcase in hand, the house was awesome and vast, as big as a lonely country inn, and except for a faint tap-tap from somewhere, mysteriously silent. A railed porch encircled it darkly. A hundred years before, five little women might have come trotting sedately down its steps. Now the house was dour, expressing the indignity of having all the velvet settees thrown away, and its insides hacked into faculty apartments. Would it still seem this way, Daisy wondered, after she had gone up this walk a hundred times and no longer saw anything? She tried thrusting herself into a future state of indifference and when this failed, considered a more direct approach, something in the nature of *Our Town*, a play she did not usually care for. House, she might say (first taking a good look around), tell me what you have in store for me. Will I be happy, will I be sad, will I one day make love on your second floor? On the third floor, which Daisy was staring at by mistake, a hand reached out to pull down a window shade. The window shade fell down altogether. A face appeared at the window, scowled fiercely, and vanished. *Mr. Rochester!* No, of course not. George Auerbach, Gorham's Poet-in-Residence. She had recognized him from his picture in the catalogue. And yet the face had been strangely frightening, almost too familiar. Recoiling a few steps, Daisy collided with a horse-faced woman who was scurrying by with a pair of binoculars swinging from her neck.

"Oh, I beg your pardon!" Daisy cried, wheeling around. "I don't usually back into people this way. It's only that I was looking up at that window and—"

"George Auerbach pulled down the shade. Don't let it worry you, my dear," the lady said, extending her hand. "Alas, it's quite character-istic—Stella Brooks."

"Daisy Lerner!"

"Oh, but of course," Mrs. Brooks said, clasping Daisy's hand warmly. "I should have known at once. My husband, Oscar Brooks, is chairman of the English department. Yes, you do look very much like the early Amelia, don't you?"

"Amelia?"

"Amelia Lacey, our poetess. Haven't you seen her grave? Oh, but I forget. You've only just arrived. Well, I'm sorry to be in such a tearing hurry just now. But I do wish you every success and happiness in Gor-ham. And needless to say, I'll be calling upon you very soon."

"Calling upon me?" Daisy said. "You mean with cards?"

"Why, yes, we used to do that, didn't we?" Mrs. Brooks remem-bered pleasantly. "We would turn down the corners if you weren't in."

Then, with a significant tap at her binoculars, she took her leave, murmuring adieu and something that sounded like tawny pippet at the end of it.

A bird watcher. Of course. Inevitable that where there was flora there would be fauna too. A mocking bird perhaps, a thrush, a grouse, or tiny pheasant. A sweet twittering began to beckon to her. Putting down Sylvia's stone-heavy suitcase, Daisy tiptoed gingerly across the dead leaves on the lawn, feeling slightly guilty about walking on the grass. The twittering drew her on irresistibly all the way around to the back of the house. She looked around her with widened eyes, realizing that she had just followed a bird into its own secret world. But what could you call this place, a grove, a garden? She had never before seen flowers growing in such profusion, or trees like these standing in the lovely timeless attitude of statues with the sunlight turning their branches into a shimmering yellow haze. The sudden beauty of it pierced her, and she finally knew what had been escaping her all day. For a moment she had a wild desire to run upstairs and write something, *anything*. Instead, she stood her ground, even when it suddenly started to rain and the first large drops plastered down her curls. Mrs. Brooks might understand what it was all about. But Daisy Lerner had just realized that she did not know the name of a single piece of nature she was looking at.

2

HIGH HEELS IN GORHAM, Tootsie Goldfarb thought, watching the girl head down the street on Tuesday morning, the first day of classes. And, in addition—she set her baby on the porch and gave a sage nod toward the small retreating figure—the strong scent of a Papa with money. Like the Gorham girls, who had arrived yesterday in time for President Steel's lawn reception and then all afternoon left their fathers standing outside the expensive stores on Main Street with open checkbooks in their hands.

Well, why not? There was no law Tootsie knew of that everyone had to start life in a dark railroad flat with an aunt who grudged every mouthful. "Right, doll?" she asked the baby, and sat down beside him, leaning back against the steps and raising her face to the hot September sun, and relishing as always the contrast between her start on the lower East Side and her present clean white establishment at Sycamore and Elm. Not, to be strictly honest about it, that Tootsie actually occupied the entire white house behind her (Edgar Dudley had installed a childless faculty couple on the top floor), and not that it was as sparkling clean on the inside as it looked from the outside. But this wasn't so important either. It was all a matter of patience. One of these days (with the help of a little buttering up) Dudley would give her a house to herself, and meanwhile before Milton came home this afternoon there would be plenty of time to take down the diapers and wipe up the cereal in this one. In fact there were moments when Tootsie felt that life had gone out of its way to teach her the beauty of patience since almost everything she had she seemed to have earned by sitting and waiting: first Milton, then her own particular piece of this clean American sunshine, and finally (after nineteen years of monthly disappointment) this little baby pasha who was bubbling away quietly in his sleep.

She leaned down to fix the strap of his sunsuit and brush a wet curl off his forehead, and then suddenly remembered how the girl had called him fat, which annoyed Tootsie although she devoted herself to keeping him that way. She had also, to be frank about it, not particularly cared for that look of surprise when she said that Milton went hunting, even though an apology had followed right afterwards. It was true that the day Milton sold his ivory chess set and bought a rifle, Tootsie had cried herself to sleep out of fear and loneliness. But Tootsie Goldfarb did not particularly like being reminded of loneliness, especially when she was sitting by herself in an empty street in Gorham with a dozen trees and a yellow bush she knew by heart.

Suddenly, on an impulse, Tootsie grabbed the baby out of the teeterbabe and gave him a big moist kiss full on the mouth. The baby started to cry and Tootsie put him back again. "Sorry doll," she murmured, swiping him under the chin with a wadded diaper as she squinted at someone else coming down the street. Who was it this time? Yes, unmistakably Babs Pilsner pulling her twins along on two tricycles tied together, a sure sign that the term was really getting under way. Babs had been up in Maine all summer, trying as usual to save her marriage, and from now until finals Tootsie would be obliged to hear all about it, including what Babs had said and what Bill had said, and what they had done together down to the very last creak of the bedsprings. Though what Babs wanted from the poor boy Tootsie would never understand, since all he wanted was to finish his dissertation in the hopes of rising higher than instructor. Her own Milton, thank god, had been an associate professor for more than two years now. As Babs came nearer, a funny smile appeared on Tootsie's face.

"Bye baby bunting," Tootsie sang, awkwardly at first and then with increasing verve, ". . . your Daddy's gone a hunting. . . ."

"But *Seymour,*" Milton Goldfarb said, beaming across the table with friendly despair, "I agree that the first few days require an adjustment. We go through this every year. But the secret of life is still work, nothing else. So what are you crapping for?"

"Milton," Seymour said reproachfully, "you should realize that what most people call laziness is a symptom of despair."

"I teach math, not philosophy," Milton said, looking despondently around the crowded coffee shop and finding it hard to believe it was the same place where all summer long he and Seymour had engaged in long murmured colloquies about the meaning of life. In August he could have heard a fly buzz around the sticky malted machine. Today the walls vibrated with the shrieks, the wails of recognition, the piercing giggles of at least a hundred packed-in undergraduates. "*Madelach, madelach,*" Milton implored them silently, "tone it down," not at all surprised when he literally failed to hear himself think. He wondered if there really had ever been a time when the proximity of just one such specimen of succulent young flesh would have sent him reeling with lust (was it George Auerbach who called them locusts on Gorham's tree of life?) because at the moment he felt as queasy as if he had gorged himself on candy before breakfast. He reminded himself that the girls were the raison d'être for the whole works, and that without them there would be no college, no courses, no teachers, ergo no Milton Goldfarb professionally employed at a life of contemplation. But the girls, perched on the counter stools, presented a whole row of plump little backsides to this notion, and in the tangle of Harvard mufflers, Bermuda shorts, and naked pink knees, he lost his train of thought altogether. Besides, Seymour was peering myopically at a corner table and no longer listening.

"Seymour—" Milton said, though he swiveled his head and raised his eyebrows with something like respect.

"A colleague," Seymour explained.

"Yeah, sure," Milton said, standing up. "Look, I have a class in a few minutes. Why don't you drop by tonight and we'll talk some more. Tootsie makes better coffee."

"Aw, come on, Milton," Seymour protested, though he continued to crane his neck past Milton's left shoulder, "a few minutes more, what difference does it make?"

Milton sighed, and partly out of good nature and partly because he hated to start forcing his way out of the place, took his seat again. He was dressed for teaching in his good dark blue suit, double-breasted and strictly non-Ivy League, and a clean white shirt which after Milton got through poking and pulling a few hours from now would go straight on back to Tootsie to be washed and ironed again.

"Frankly," he said, "in my opinion you ask too much out of life. You don't pay enough attention to the positive side. For example, number one—home life. You have a marvelous wife, right?"

"Right," Seymour agreed absently. "The best."

"Fine," Milton nodded. "So that's number one, and the greatest blessing, believe me. Not to mention your four, healthy, strapping, snotty-nosed children, they should live and be well—"

"*Hel-lo!*" Seymour mouthed, suddenly popping up and waving through the crowd.

"Seymour—" Milton repeated, and then when Seymour had subsided again, shrugged and added, "—okay. So maybe right there is your answer. Maybe a little, shall we say, adventure on the side is just what you need to shake yourself up. I mean, god knows *I* don't have the time for something like that, not to mention energy, but you, Seymour, you're a big healthy type—"

"You don't seem to understand what a fine person Julia is," Seymour murmured to the distance, clearing his throat. "You have to remember I don't deserve her."

"That's right," Milton nodded, "I keep forgetting." He drummed his fingers in a slow tired tattoo on the tabletop. "Listen, have you ever seriously considered sports?" he said. "It's true Tootsie cried when I traded in the chess set, but I tell you those mornings when Dudley comes over at the crack of dawn—"

"Dudley is a shit."

"So *my* refrigerator happens to work," Milton said. "Seymour, I really must go. Why don't you just take a tip from George Auerbach and apply your ass to the seat of the chair? Rain or shine, that guy's at it."

Seymour wrenched himself around. "Now, don't hand me that shit about Auerbach," he said, warming up to the subject for the first time. "Two crap courses and the guy thinks he's god around here—when he's here. All he's got to worry about is his goddamn sinuses. Hell, who wouldn't be creative with a deal like that? No paper work, a ready-made reputation, and divorced besides. I'd like to see *him* produce with a wife and four kids and—"

Milton stared out at the tangle of honey-colored females where Seymour's colleague was ensconced between two tittering freshmen.

"Seymour," Milton sighed gently, "George never told you to fuck your wife."

". . . gosh, Miss Lerner," the intense redhead with the white eyebrows was saying, "it was awfully kind of you to have this coffee with us."

"On the contrary, Doris," Daisy smiled, "the pleasure was all mine."

"*She's* Doris. I'm Leslie."

"Sorry."

"—and we certainly found the class hour very wonderful and stimulating too. Especially what you said about having to enlarge our horizons and broaden our perspectives."

"I think," Daisy said, putting down her cup and trying to remember, "that it was the other way around, wasn't it?"

"Was it? Oh *god*, I'd better fix up my notes. But then I mean, in addition to teaching—" She paused to allow large-faced Doris to join her in a rapturous exhalation "—to publish all those stories in *The New Yorker* and everything."

"Well, I can't claim to have published anything in *The New Yorker* exactly," Daisy said. "I only mentioned that I did recently get an awfully sweet note from them."

"But that's absolutely fantastic! And then to be the author of all those books too!"

"One short novel," Daisy corrected her gently, "merely one—and very short," and succeeded in precipitating both girls into such a tizzy of admiration that she wondered guiltily where she had misled them.

The crowd in the coffee shop seemed to be thinning out a little. Even that pale but friendly young man from the English department who had been staring at her over his friend, had approached on the verge of speech, shaken his head, and departed. She looked at the clock in the corner and stood up. It was almost three, the hour when Professor Brooks had asked her at the President's reception to stop by at his office. On either side of her, the two freshmen rose up also, only about eighteen years old but already so gigantic that as they made their way out she was a tiny pea between two mattresses. How strange. In all her fantasies about dedicating herself to the young, Daisy had never expected her first students to shrink her. But on the other hand, the girls were also very admiring and respectful, even of her clothes, which they had commented on along with everything else. ("I just love the yellow of that blouse, Miss Lerner." "Thank you.")

"Oh, and by the way," a suddenly emboldened Doris (Leslie?) gig-gled as they emerged on Main Street, looking down on her like a huge puppy dog awed by a clever mouse, "we were wondering if you were ever a Gorham girl yourself."

"Me a Gorham girl?" Daisy said. "God, no."

"Smith? Radcliffe?"

"Actually, I went to school right in New York," Daisy said, and watched as with a pair of very muted oh's and dimmed smiles, Doris and Leslie bounded off, blazers flying, as if they were hoping, poor things, to shed this pall that had suddenly been cast on them.

With a thoughtful shrug, Daisy crossed the busy traffic island and entered the campus. The library where Professor Brooks shared an office with a valuable butterfly collection and where she had been assigned a desk in the stacks was one of the largest college buildings, heavily gabled and turreted against Gothic invasion and at this season also protected by a thick shiny layer of red ivy. As she saw it looming in the distance, Daisy suddenly thought of her own apartment back on Elm Street. It had been very unrealistic, she could see that now, to expect Mr. Dudley to furnish her with a rosewood escritoire, chrysan-themums in muted silver bowls and beautifully aged chintzes (herself presiding in black with pearls). Still it had been an undeniable shock to walk into a twin of the summer bungalow Mrs. Lerner had rented in the mountains when Mr. Lerner was having that bad year in the fur business. Was it possible that all academic housing ran in this direction? Over by the little art museum, two neat young men were putting bicycle clips around their trousers. She had seen them at the reception yesterday and heard them say they roomed together, but not where. She had also met a Miss Gabrielle Hochmeister, who had evidently been hired to teach French with a German accent, but Gabrielle had a faculty room in one of the dormitories and kept a hot plate and an ironing board in the bathroom, so that was no help either.

At the foot of the stone steps leading to the library, she stopped and looked around. It had been raining on and off ever since her arrival, but the latest cloudburst this morning had yielded a day so brilliant that puddles and all, Gorham College looked just like its calendar picture in the bookstore with its iron gates and the vivid autumn foliage of the hills beyond. There was a fresh smell of winesap and pine needles in the air, and overhead a pleasant activity among the birds, who hopped from sodden branch to branch, sending down a sparkling shower each time they landed. Lights were on in many of the buildings, feeble against the sunshine, and clusters of big girls leaned against their bicycles quietly chatting with each other. A poignant mixture of overgrown youth and nature. Suddenly, terribly glad she had come to Gorham in spite of everything, Daisy pulled herself together, trying to make up a list like the one in *The Great Gatsby*: 1—Make apartment charming; 2—Get extra lamb chops, also caviar in case of company; 3—learn to drive(?); 4—Meet life here head-on *somehow*; 5—? But she had already hung herself up on number 4, wondering if she ought to include in this category long walks on twittering country roads, illustrated bird books, etc. And why not? she asked herself, taking another breath of that clear clean air that made every problem seem to have a solution. Hadn't Faulkner himself insisted that man would not only endure, he would prevail? An exhilarating idea, until a voice behind her said:

"Screaming at Charlie. Now why the hell would you want to do a thing like that?"

She turned. A man with a moist whisky-red face was shaking his head at her in a strangely intimate reproach.

"Edgar Dudley. Basketball and housing."

"Oh—how do you do."

"Screaming at Charlie," he repeated. "When all he wanted to do was put up that storm window outside of your bathroom."

"I appreciate that fact, Mr. Dudley—"

"Edgar."

"Edgar—but unfortunately I was trying to take a bath at the time."

"You New Yorkers. Always acting as if somebody's going to murder you in your sleep, not that I blame you—coming from that town. Now, tell you what you do—" He gave her a quick ruddy wink, making all Daisy's previous sins, whatever their nature, a private matter between them, "—the first thing is, forget all about New York. This is a different type of community with a different type of person. Get what I mean? Or haven't you met any of the folks yet?"

"Well, not as many as I'd hoped, frankly," Daisy said. "But let's see. I was introduced to Gabrielle Hochmeister at the reception yesterday, and oh yes, Mrs. Goldfarb the day before that, who—"

"Tootsie," Edgar Dudley said. "Yeah, well some people find it hard to make any kind of adjustment. But not you. I can see from the looks of you you're a real smart kid. Just get with it and you'll be fine. How do you like your apartment, by the way? Real sweet place, isn't it? You were damned lucky I managed to get it for you."

"Really? Well, maybe after I've fixed it up a little—"

"No, no," Edgar Dudley said. "I don't have any time for *that*. This season of the year not a damn thing gets done around here without my making sure it does. I'll just send a man over to check on that sink and also the refrigerator. By the way, anything I can do for you in the way of appliances?"

"No, not at the moment."

"Okay, nobody's asking you to make any hasty decisions. Take your time, think it over. When you decide, let me know. There's a guy in town just happens to owe me a few favors."

"I'll bet he does."

"Ho, ho, ho!" Edgar Dudley cried, convulsed with mirth. "That's okay. I like a girl with a sense of humor. Yessir, you'll do all right here. Just hang around with the right people, get active with Stella Brooks in the Ladies of Gorham and you'll be fine. You're going to Stella's tea for the newcomers this afternoon, aren't you?"

"Am I?"

"Sure. Grand bunch of girls, the Ladies of Gorham—they can do a lot for you."

"Do I want them to?"

"Listen, little lady, remember this: Gorham's a damn friendly place to anybody who wants to be friendly. But if you're going to start out being a lone ranger—"

"Oh, please don't worry about me, Mr. Dudley."

"Edgar."

"Edgar. After all," Daisy said gaily, "if it doesn't work out here I can always leave."

"Leave *Gorham*?" Edgar Dudley cried, jovially slapping her on the shoulder. "Nobody ever leaves Gorham," and walked away, still chuckling at the thought.

The huge studded doors clanged behind her loudly, causing the librarian at the other end of the marble floor to look up and stare. A few girls wandered about in silent sneakers, and the thick gray pillars rose noiselessly towards the vaulted ceiling. The librarian looked around once more and then returned to the important process of stamping books for a patient female professor with a wispy bun and a concave bosom who seemed to be held together by a few bits of heirloom lace and string. Her name was Miss Badger, a specialist in Romantic literature. They had trotted her out yesterday to greet the new faculty and trotted her back again, smiling diffusely the whole time. As Gabrielle Hochmeister approached from the reading room, Daisy ducked behind a pillar and read a few notices she had already seen. One of them was an urgent appeal from the Hillel society for new members; another, rather more delicately phrased, invited her to a reading of some original verse by Mrs. Stella Brooks, who seemed to be a sort of local poetess as well as the president of the Ladies of Gorham. As she got to the notice about a Mr. William Atkinson who would deliver a series of mid-winter seminars on "Innocence in Jeopardy," Daisy raised her eyes. With a sudden ferocious clatter of footsteps, a short very handsome man darted from the stacks to the card file and proceeded to flip through one drawer after the next, slamming each one in turn and frowning like a celebrity, which by local standards he certainly was. Her first night she had unpacked almost hypnotized by that fraught, slightly sinister tap, tap, tap overhead, until when the sound suddenly ceased at ten she realized that George Auerbach wrote his poems on a typewriter. Otherwise, unfortunately, he was not much in evidence. Yesterday at the reception all the freshmen had been clustered around the punch bowl hoping that he would come, and when she left the punch was down to a few blobs of sherbet and they were still clustered. She herself had only spoken to him once, and even then she could not claim that it had been in her own person exactly since it was on the steps of 69 Elm Street this morning where he had pinched her behind and asked her to wait for his laundry. Therefore, among other things, one might assume that he was just another absent-minded professor, or that details did not interest him and let it go at that. And yet . . .

"Shouldn't you have graduated by now?" George Auerbach turned to murmur, looking into her face with a puzzled frown.

"Very soon," Daisy whispered back, their lips an inch apart.

With a nod, he slammed the drawer back into place and vanished into the stacks.

Daisy looked after him pensively. And yet, and yet . . . there was something thrilling about the man. Not just his reputation, or his gifts, or his handsome looks, which considering that he was a practicing intellectual were almost extraordinary, with that half-Greek half-Jewish nose and chin, and crisp black hair and cocky solid build of a bantam-weight. And not even his elusiveness, or the fact that the picture for the catalogue had evidently been taken on the day when he wandered into someone else's class by mistake, lectured brilliantly for an hour, and wandered out again without ever knowing the difference. No—from the stacks there came a huge crash and some language that momentarily paralyzed Miss Badger in her lace—no, it was something more important, something to do with the fact that only George Auerbach ever made any noise in the library.

* * *

Professor Brooks stopped making a church out of his fingers and tapping his nose with the steeple long enough to assist Daisy to a seat.

"Not," he added, resuming his own place behind the desk, "that I will be taking up much of your time. I only wished, as I believe I stated at the President's house yesterday, to extend my personal greetings, and also give you a few extra copies of the curriculum—which happen to be right here."

He handed Daisy a sheaf of mimeographed papers and sat back, well satisfied, his lean bald head warmed by the dying sunlight, and the glass cases full of pretty butterflies glinting on either side of him.

"It's awfully good of you," Daisy assured him, craning her neck back towards the main library several times before turning around for good, "very kind indeed—oh, what an *interesting* office!"

"Thank you."

"Though it must be awfully disturbing to see them all pinioned."

"The butterflies?" Professor Brooks said, smiling indulgently. "They're quite dead, I'm afraid."

"Caught and preserved by experts," Daisy nodded. "Who would want to be an expert on *anything*, I sometimes ask myself. . . ." Her voice faltered slightly. "I beg your pardon. Your own field is Early Middle English, I believe?"

"Not at all, not at all," Professor Brooks said, waving away her apologies. "The fiery enthusiasms of youth. I recall the selfsame qualities in myself."

"I'm sure you do," Daisy said.

"Yes," Professor Brooks repeated. "Yes—well, now, tell me how you got on with your classes today. Do you think you can handle them?"

"I don't see why not," Daisy said. "They're peculiarly tall, but otherwise friendly enough."

"Good, I'm glad to hear it—about the friendliness, I mean. I'm sorry, incidentally, that we weren't able to give you more than a desk in the stacks for the present, but owing to evermore crowded conditions—"

"No, no," Daisy assured him, "I feel that the library offers me immense possibilities."

"Fine. And your domestic accommodations are equally satisfactory?"

"Well," Daisy said, crossing her legs and tugging on the thin wool skirt at her knees, "Mr. Dudley seems to think I'm lucky to have them."

"Then I'm sure you are," Professor Brooks said. "Which isn't to say that those of us who have chosen to put down our roots here aren't more substantially housed. My wife and I, for example, have chosen to build—far out in the country—I hope, by the way, that you'll honor us with a little visit one of these days?"

"With great pleasure."

"—the pleasure will be ours—and perhaps our little home will interest you from an architectural point of view. But I can assure you, Miss Lerner, that when we first came here twenty years ago we took pot luck with everyone else. Or perhaps the fact that your little apartment is less than luxurious doesn't seriously concern you? Perhaps you already miss the hurly burly and glitter of the great metropolis?"

"I have left New York far behind me," Daisy said firmly. "For the present."

"Ah? Then teaching interests you that much? I was afraid that perhaps you saw your vocation as that of the, uh—lady novelist. Because, speaking frankly, Miss Lerner, I must tell you now that Gorham is not likely to further any personal literary ambitions. We are only a small teaching college and all we ask of our teachers is that they teach. As to the rest of it—the 'moment of truth'—we tend to leave that sort of thing to the Church, or possibly Harvard."

"That's very funny," Daisy laughed.

"What? Yes, it is, isn't it?" Professor Brooks said, smiling with a kind of relief until Daisy leaned forward in her low-necked yellow blouse to flip through the curriculum, and with a slight cough he swiveled his chair, so that his next remarks were addressed to an old wooden filing cabinet in the corner, overflowing with exam papers.

"Miss Lerner—" portentous pause "—I think I'd better be honest with you. Before you came in, I happen to have been looking over your academic record again, and though it's all very well as far as it goes—"

"You're trying to tell me it doesn't go far enough," Daisy said, looking up.

"Exactly!"

Professor Brooks swiveled around again, touching a precautionary hand to his mouth for a moment before he continued.

"Look here, Miss Lerner, much as we pride ourselves on our liberal hiring policies, we must insist on certain assurances in return, you know. The promise of work towards a doctorate, certainly a start on a master's. Now unfortunately in *your* case, immediately following your graduation the record goes blank—except for a course or two at the New School, and your inclusion in that anthology."

"And the English department doesn't approve of anthologies?"

"Of course it does," Professor Brooks said testily. "All of us in the department are very much engaged with them." He smiled, still a little testily. "You might even say they constitute the very fabric of our lives. In fact, I myself happen to be the editor of several, whose nature and contents I won't bore you with now. And your own little novelette, which I have just had the pleasure of reading—"

"Oh?"

"—while surprisingly modest in its intention, testifies to an obvious talent."

"Thank you."

"Indeed, you mustn't think you're the only member of our faculty who happens to be creative. Far from it. There's our own George Auerbach, Mrs. Carp of the French department, who specializes in cookbooks, my wife—and so on. But generally these are older people, wise to the ways of academic life. Whereas you, who are just starting out, and with no promise of graduate work to come—" Professor Brooks laughed, hoping, he soon saw vainly, that Daisy might join him again, "—well, how do we know the muses won't speak to you in the midst of Freshman Composition I?"

"They won't."

"All right," Professor Brooks said, nodding amiably. "I didn't expect you to see the dangers now. Anymore than I would expect you to—" The sight of Daisy crossing her legs and on the verge of leaning forward again finished the comparison, "—well, to be apprehensive about your appearance."

"My appearance?" Daisy said with surprise. "You find me unkempt?"

"On the contrary. To resort to a colloquialism, very neat indeed. Oh, come now, Miss Lerner, why such astonishment? Surely the fact that you are a very lovely young woman has affected your life before this?"

"You're kind to put it that way," Daisy murmured, "but this is a *girls'* school."

"And we regard our girls as very tender charges."

"But my dear Professor Brooks," Daisy said, "if you take away how I look and then subtract the fact that I've written a short novel—a long short story—what's left of me? Practically nothing."

"Nothing?" Professor Brooks said. "Surely you exaggerate."

"Do I?" Daisy asked.

She stared at him intensely. There was a sudden boom of thunder and as Daisy's eyes widened, the sun went out completely, yielding to a torrent of thick black rain. Through the open window, a fragile beech tree shrank away from the wind, losing its copper leaves to the storm.

"You see?" Daisy cried over the downpour. "A pathetic fallacy!"

"Nonsense," Professor Brooks retorted. "You have a tendency to the dramatic, Miss Lerner, which you really ought to try to curb."

He got up and began working rapidly in the gloom, as one accustomed to it, deftly distributing paperweights over his desk, slamming the window shut, and clicking on the overhead light, an opaque white globe hanging from an iron rod in the ceiling.

"We are in a valley," he said. "This kind of thing happens all the time. It has no symbolic value whatsoever."

"I see," Daisy said, and since Professor Brooks remained standing, got up also.

"It was good of you to come in, Miss Lerner. I hope you will feel free to come in again, any time."

"Thank you."

"And do take heart," Professor Brooks smiled. "If you feel I've been too harsh with you today, try to understand that I only meant to spare you disappointment in the future."

"I understand."

"Come now, Miss Lerner, all places are lonely at the beginning.

Aren't they? . . . Look here, you'll be seeing my wife at the tea later on. And before long, well I'm sure she'll be calling on you—"

"With cards," Daisy said. "She said something about you turn down the corners if I'm not in."

"—calling on you," Professor Brooks repeated, as if there had been no interruption, "to give a little talk for the Ladies of Gorham,"—and guiding Daisy's elbow with surprising gentleness, escorted her out the door.

3

ALL AROUND IN THE DUSK the girls were swarming home and Elm Street stretched dim and depleted, except for the great well-lit houses which glowed and beckoned like other people's homes passed on a speeding train at night. "*Au revoir!*" Gabrielle Hochmeister called, pausing to wave under the lantern-lit porte cochère of her dormitory. "And don't forget—*à bientôt!*"

"*À bientôt,*" Daisy nodded, listlessly lifting a briefcase in which two small rib lamb chops were resting against approximately seventy-five freshman themes. The tea for the newcomers had been very nice. The two boys from the art department had asked her to come to Provincetown this summer, and Mrs. Brooks had indeed invited her to make a little speech ("Only about ten minutes long, of absolutely no consequence," she had explained, giggling diffidently). And Gabrielle Hochmeister, in addition to expressing the hope that Daisy would come to dinner on Faculty Night, had told her more about the hot plate and the ironing board in her bathroom. For a moment as she paused at the foot of Tootsie Goldfarb's walk in time to see Tootsie Goldfarb smile through the window like a jack o'lantern and whip the curtains closed, Daisy toyed with the possibility of buying some knee socks and Bermuda shorts of her own and disguising herself as an undergraduate. Not a feasible idea—she seemed to have aged so much within a few days, but flickeringly enticing: girlish laughter and giggling, hamburgers dripping down the chin at midnight, racing to answer the telephone as curlers clacked in her hair. ". . . Daisy! Daisy! It's for *you* again! . . ." Ah. Unfortunately, 69 Elm Street had already loomed into sight, glowering at the end of its long cracked path like that house in *Wuthering Heights*. The light in the third-floor window cast its usual doleful yellow gleam, except that a curious shadow play seemed to be taking place behind the window shade (Had he put it back up again? It was always being wrenched at, and crashing down), as if a hand, yet not a hand, were scratching away at the air. A *paw*, Daisy might almost have said, if she had not known better—or did she?

The interview with Professor Brooks suddenly came back into her mind in all its painfully vivid detail—he had called her back afterwards to give her the few extra copies of the curriculum, which she appeared to have forgotten—and she could hardly deny that she had made a complete ass of herself. And yet, a part of her still refused to acknowledge that she was wrong and he was right. After all, why couldn't it be the other way around? She mounted the creaking porch steps, her feet brushed by the dried tendrils of last year's ivy, and thoughtfully pushed open the heavily protesting storm door. Then, still deep in contemplation, she paused in the dimly lit vestibule and looked up the slippery wooden stairs that led to her apartment. There was that sound again, like a faint but compelling woodpecker, tapping out the distant fascinating possibility that everybody was out of step but Daisy Lerner. It was all so clear: hup, two, three, four, a battalion in full battle dress about-faced—while Daisy promptly wheeled around in the opposite direction. A second barked command—and this time, Daisy marched right off the field all by herself. But why not? In lots of movies as well as novels it often turned out that only the isolated fool had caught the word. A staggering idea, now that she was giving heed to all its implications. She saw a prophet moaning in the wilderness, she saw him shaking a fist at the voice of the Lord. Alas, she also saw him being asked, quite politely, for some sort of evidence that God had spoken to him in the first place. With a low whistle, Daisy started quickly up the stairs.

At first the sweaty key refused to budge the lock. An almost hysterical moment later, Daisy turned the knob smoothly and realized that the door had been open all the time. She flicked on the lights, sniffing and peering around her like a castaway on a strange, possibly hostile island. No one had gotten there ahead of her this time. Good. She was tired of finding Edgar Dudley's henchmen all over the place, and remembered his wheezy assurance that she was lucky to have this apartment at all. There was no doubt in her mind by now that whoever furnished it also designed bomb shelters, since no one else could possibly have calculated the minimum needs of a single human being to such a nicety. In the living room, which was a simple square, there was exactly one of everything, no more, no less: one blue chintz sofa with a tilting bridge lamp to guard it, one small desk of orange maple, one red peeling armchair, a lumpy card table and—aha! the first chink in the system—*two* dime-store ashtrays. Over in the corner a set of Toulouse-Lautrec prints and a hammer still lay on the floor where Daisy had abandoned them that morning after having achieved several large holes in the plaster.

The kitchen, to which she presently brought her lamb chops and a sinking heart, seemed a little friendlier, perhaps because it smelled faintly of the farmyard. Hungry for some warmth, she turned on the burners of the bandy-legged stove, undoubtedly one of the first electric models, and peered into the waist-high refrigerator, which was ticking away like an agonized cricket. A bottle of milk gleamed on the bare shelf. It had a note around its neck from someone who called himself Daisy's friendly milkman and said he would come again soon. The note moved her strangely. Holding it against her breast, she went on into the bedroom, which was the bleakest part of the apartment and since it was also stripped to its barest essentials, something of a personal insult. She sat down on her bony bed, unable to get a clear image of herself in the streaky mirror. Which was it today? Harpo Marx? Shirley Temple? A touch of the poet? It had grown very dark. Outside the rain began again, fragrantly beating on the sodden leaves of a hemlock tree, mingling memory with desire. But could love, not to say lust, live in such a place? The bedsprings poked insidiously at her small buttocks, inviting her to become an old maid and die in her sleep and not be discovered for three days. It was the merest suggestion, but enough to make Daisy's heart flutter wildly, like an imprisoned young bird. No, no! She was not meant to live alone. Give her back the bright lights and laughter. Give her back New York. *Oh, my New York, my New York.* The words tolled like a bell, mingling ominously with other noises in the background. A door opening and closing, footsteps on a creaking wooden floor. She believed in ghosts. On the other hand, she had seen the plumbers with her own eyes. Or maybe this time it was a visit from Edgar Dudley himself. She stood up, trembling with purpose. "Mr. Dudley," she planned to say, "village custom or not, I *urge* you to think about this in terms of the Bill of Rights."

But, "Oh," Daisy actually said. "It's only you."

"I was in the neighborhood, so I thought I'd drop in," Seymour Lipshansky explained with a sheepish grin, already halfway into her living room with his skinny body folded in the general direction of her sofa. The hand reaching for the zipper on his tan windbreaker arrested itself, and he gave her a sudden reproachful look through his pale eyeglasses.

"—what do you mean, only me?"

"Please don't take it the way it sounds. It's just that for a minute there I thought you were Edgar Dudley."

"That shit," Seymour said.

"Yes."

"Everybody around here hates him," Seymour assured her. "Did I scare you?"

"No, not really. I think maybe I'm getting used to finding people inside."

"But it's nothing like New York, is it?" Seymour said.

"Oh? Are you a New Yorker too?"

"Christ no," Seymour said, as if the very thought exhausted him. "If I even have to go to that jungle for the MLA convention, I beat it back as fast as I can. It's just a goddamn rat race. All that competition and backbiting, and not even a decent yard for the kids to play in."

"I don't have any kids," Daisy said.

"You will," Seymour assured her grimly.

"Yes," Daisy sighed. "I suppose so . . . look, can you stay a while? Why don't you make yourself at home and I'll get you a can of beer."

"Beer?" Seymour said, as if the idea were novel but not impossible. "Okay, why not?"

The can which Daisy brought back was sharp and frosty to the touch. It was also her last, a point that she hoped Seymour would not make an issue of. But if he noticed that she had nothing left for herself, he did not mention it, partly because he seemed to be so busy following her instructions about making himself at home to the letter, that he had already stripped the windbreaker off his tattered navy blue sweater, and stretched himself out on her couch as well as his length permitted, so that his head was propped up on one of its arms, and his feet in a pair of ancient pointy shoes fell over the other. Aside from a few circus clowns, she had never seen anyone go limp so quickly. Was he this relaxed with other people, Daisy wondered, or did she have some special effect on him?

"I have four, you know," Seymour remarked, taking a long slurp from the beer can and setting it carefully on the floor.

"Four what?"

"Four kids."

"Wow."

"Yeah. And a wife and—ah, what the hell. Why even bother to gas about it?" He gave his head a mild half-turn and regarded her sympathetically. "You look kind of bushed yourself. What's the matter? Not enough sack time?"

"The way things are going," Daisy said, slumping into her armchair, "I'll clock up enough sack time for an army."

"But you're depressed about something," Seymour said. "It's all that paper work, I bet. That's all you get around here. They tell you they're hiring you as a teacher and then it turns out they meant file clerk." Seymour slipped off his glasses and rubbed tiredly at the bridge of his nose. "It's like their other crap about the big liberal policy. Come join our beautiful community, work for coolie wages, and instructors and minorities stay out in left field where you belong."

"Really?" Daisy said. "It's true that I only seem to get introduced to—"

"Not, you understand, that this goes for certain big shots like gorgeous George up there," Seymour continued as Daisy stiffened in her chair "—who's probably got his nose in the vaporizer right this minute." He gestured at the ceiling with his glasses, his eyes naked and bitter. "Oh, no. For him all bets are off. He's the one they put in the catalogue. He's the one they show off to the world."

"Maybe they think he's exotic," Daisy said, warming up to the subject, only to find that Seymour had already slid by it.

"Whereas, they see a guy like me coming and right away they lower the boom."

"Boom," Daisy echoed sadly, as the vision of George Auerbach evaporated again.

"Oh, well, that's life," Seymour said, fishing around in his pants pocket for a pipe. He took a few sucks at the stem, which made a hollow mournful sound, and then began a series of little futile clutching gestures at his body.

"I think," Seymour said with an embarrassed smile, "that I left my tobacco home."

"Would you like a cigarette?"

"Okay, why not?"

She tossed him the crumpled pack, from which Seymour took a cigarette and lit it with a borrowed match. Then he lay back, puffing contentedly, while the two of them watched the smoke slowly rising, Daisy with an increasingly wistful eye since like the beer it was the last one in the house and she could hardly run out on a dark country street to look for more. *Schnorrer*, she told herself automatically. But for all its aptness, the word failed to cling. No, there was no denying that Seymour had a decided appeal, a certain plaintiveness that was drawing them closer and closer each minute he stayed. Watch it, Daisy. You're just feeling lonesome. Remember, this type is always poison for you. But her heart was finding it harder and harder to resist. An orphan, probably. Yes, a waif, eternally last on line for soup. She saw him vividly with his sleeves shrunk up to his elbows, and skinny ankles sticking out of his pants. She yearned to ladle everything out to him. "Daisy?" he was saying, "*Daisy . . .*"

"Yes!"

"Gee, you have pretty hair."

"Oh, why thank you."

"So nice and blond and fluffy. It makes you look a little bit like Shirley Temple. Lots of people tell you that?"

"A few."

"Watch out for the wolves around here."

"I will."

The shadow that had been hovering over Seymour's vulnerable young face grew even darker. Daisy realized that he was looking at the uncovered typewriter on her desk.

"I understand you write?"

"Just one short novel and please let's not talk about it now."

"One short novel doesn't mean anything."

"I know it."

"Neither does one short story."

"No?"

"I had a story published once. It was about my father. Any of the big magazines would have taken it, but I sent it to the *Paducah Review*. I didn't want my father to see it."

"Did he?"

"My uncle found it on a newsstand and showed it to him. When he read it, he came to me crying. Imagine it, a grown man with the tears streaming down his face."

"Oh, Seymour, that's terrible."

"Why?" Seymour asked defensively. "Why shouldn't I have painted an honest picture of him? You think I owe that lousy bastard anything?"

"You don't?"

"Listen, you don't know how he treated my mother and me when I was a kid, you don't know how he kept us locked up on that lousy farm of his." Seymour's face brightened suddenly. "Oh, that's right. I forgot to tell you. I was brought up on a farm—right in this valley, as a matter of fact. Then I went to Yale."

"Was *Yale* nice?" Daisy asked hopefully.

"Are you kidding? They all thought I was one of those rich Jewish playboys."

"And you're not rich."

"I'm not even Jewish. My father was a Pole. My mother was Ukrainian. And don't think my father let her forget it either. He made her life miserable. Dumb Ukrainian, he called her—right up to the day she died."

"The brute," Daisy said. "No wonder you wrote that story about him."

"That's no excuse," Seymour corrected her. "There's never any excuse for hurting people. Not," Seymour added with a bitter smile, "that he didn't make *my* life sheer hell. He never let me off that damn farm. We had plenty of money for hired help, but I was always kept home from school at harvest time. I never had one single playmate."

"Listen, this is heartbreaking," Daisy said.

"I used to talk to the cows. I used to get out of my bed at night and sleep in the barn just to be near something warm."

"My god, you poor darling."

"The day my mother died, he told me she'd killed herself because she hated the sight of me."

"Oh, he *didn't!*" Daisy cried. "He *couldn't.* Why, Seymour—" he had sat up and was squinting at her abjectly "—Seymour, what's the matter?"

"I can't see you from over here. I'm nearsighted."

"Of course you are," Daisy said passionately, "of course you are."

She ran over to sit beside him, and Seymour immediately locked his arms around her waist and buried his face in her lap. "You poor, poor thing," Daisy said, stroking his thin pale hair, while Seymour all muffled and bereft repeated, "Oh god, was I lonesome, was I lonesome . . ."

The barking of the dogs and the cheery voice calling out, "Hello, hello, anybody home?" shot them apart like a bolt of electricity. They stared at each other with naked horror—Seymour, in fact, reached automatically for his fly—and then turned stricken eyes to the visitor (three visitors, if two large bounding poodles were counted in), a woman in a raincoat and a striped college muffler who was only too obviously, *Mrs.* Seymour Lipshansky.

"Now look," Daisy said, getting up by shoving Seymour down

(*sauve qui peut*), "whatever you're thinking, I assure you I can explain it to your satisfaction."

"Gracious," Julia said, laughing mildly, "what am I supposed to be thinking?"

"Ah, thank god," Daisy murmured, "the civilized kind. Please do come in. I'm pleased to meet you."

"We've already met," Julia smiled, "at President Steel's reception. I was helping serve."

"Oh, yes," Daisy said, vaguely remembering an overage Gorhamite with a barrette in her hair and a tidy string of cultured pearls. The fresh air certainly made a difference. This one looked as if she had come bounding through the streets breathing deeply the whole way, all flushed and energetic like the dogs who were leaping up and slurping on either side of her.

"How sweet," Julia said, glancing around and fending off her animals with a helpless laugh. "Did Edgar Dudley find you this? All maple and chintz. It reminds me of my undergraduate days."

"How did you know I was here?" Seymour said morosely.

"I saw the car outside. Can she come on the tenth, by the way?"

"I don't know. There wasn't time to ask her."

"Really, darling," Julia said, and turned to Daisy with faintly amused exasperation. "Seymour was supposed to ask you to dinner if he saw you," she explained. "I hope you can make it. Nothing special. Just a few people you might like to meet. George Auerbach, maybe, unless you see too much of him as it is."

"No, in fact I—"

"Everybody's always fascinated with George," Julia smiled. "I hope you won't be disappointed. Oh, these dogs! Coming now, Seymour, or are you staying a while?"

"Well, maybe," Seymour said. "Maybe I'll just have one more beer."

"You drank the last one," Daisy said.

"I did?"

"Come on, darling," Julia laughed, "let's leave this poor girl alone. I can tell the dogs are annoying her."

"I'm just not used to animals," Daisy smiled. "I was brought up in the city."

"Were you? What a shame. Coming, Seymour?"

Daisy closed the door after them, leaning against it and murmuring "good-bye" and "thank you" for several moments after they had left, until she realized that people only did that in the movies. But, ah, an invitation to someone's house and a chance to meet George Auerbach. She crossed the small living room, ignoring the mashed-in sofa, the toppled can of beer, the Lautrec prints waiting to be hung, and flung the window open wide. The night air was damp and smelled of earth. Down below, her first guests—though pride had kept her from telling them so—filed out of the house as silhouettes against a silver moon, Julia striding ahead briskly with the dogs jumping up on either side of her, Seymour loping a few steps behind with shoulders hunched and beak thrust forward. Daisy thought of her next letter to Sylvia. ("Dinner party . . . neighbors . . . went out of their way to be friendly . . .) Out of their way? An odd thought buzzed through from one ear to the other. Yes, very odd. For the Lipshanskys had definitely gone home on foot and the car that Julia said she had seen outside had never been there.

That night, tossing in a lumpy bed, Daisy dreamed of passionately kissing William Holden and of eternity. A tiny bird was flying back and forth, piling up infinite dunes of sand one grain at a time. In her sleep, Daisy staggered on through the desert, throat parched, wondering if Tootsie Goldfarb would ever stop smiling and ask her in for coffee, and when William Holden finally materialized to take her in his arms, he was wearing the khaki uniform of the Afrika Corps. "Gorham is the friendliest place in the world!" he suddenly boomed like a foghorn. "Just get into step and you'll never want to leave." "But I can't even find the parade!" Daisy cried—and sat up in bed with a start.

4

EVIDENTLY, the Lipshanskys had not so much moved into their house as stolen into it one night with a few sticks of furniture and claimed squatters' rights. It was all so bare and unfinished that even the harlequin design of the curtains was unraveling itself at the edges, and amid the many objects abandoned by the Lipshansky children, which were all clearly visible from the doorway of the living room—a dismantled kiddie car lying among its several pieces on the floor, a fire truck, a small jungle gym, and assorted sweaters and gloves—there was even a leftover child, a tiny boy in drop-seat pajamas who was being feverishly pawed by a huge dog. But if Julia had any intention of rescuing him, she gave no sign of it, and neither did the other guests who were standing around drinking whisky out of cheese glasses, including, yes! George Auerbach, who was intently picking the cheese out of his.

"Well, don't *you* look nice," Julia Lipshansky said, tossing Daisy's fur jacket on a pile of tangled snowsuits and rubbers behind her at which another huge dog was sniffing eagerly. "I'm afraid you're going to think we're all terribly inelegant here. None of us can afford furs—" she laughed "—except the undergraduates."

"My father's a furrier."

"Oh, is he?" Julia said, raising her hands to her hair as a hole gaped under each armpit. "How sweet," and led Daisy into the group.

"Well, *hi*," Seymour grinned, rushing over with a depleted whisky bottle and an unsteady tower of glasses against his chest. "Have a drink."

"Thank you," Daisy said, holding the other glasses for him as he poured it out.

"And could I have a little more seltzer when you're finished, maybe?" Tootsie Goldfarb asked.

"Oh, good evening, Mrs. Goldfarb."

"Dear me," Julia laughed. "I've just realized you don't know everyone here. Let's see now, you've met Tootsie, of course, and Seymour. . . . This is Milton Goldfarb—" she indicated a short, bushy-haired man who smiled amiably.

"How do you do."

"—and George Auerbach, whom you were so anxious to get to know. For goodness sakes, George, say hello to the girl."

"Hello," George Auerbach said, blowing his nose, and further obliging Julia by looking Daisy over from head to toe. "Who's your favorite novelist?" he asked her bosom.

"Dickens."

"That's interesting," he said, draining off the rest of his drink. "For the last few years it's been nothing earlier than Salinger."

"Oh, for Christ's sake," Seymour said.

"You mustn't mind him, doll," Tootsie Goldfarb explained confidentially, sitting down on the sofa with a whooshing sound as Daisy joined her.

"Who?" Daisy asked, taking a sip and coughing slightly.

"Georgie over there. It's the books. He's busy with them all the time. It makes him nervous. My husband is the same way."

"Tootsie," Milton laughed.

Tootsie smiled at him, but with the painful brightness of an oncoming headlight. She was a changed person from the one Daisy usually passed on the porch, no longer comfortably spread out in the sunshine, but very much a company Tootsie. She kept making decorous adjustments to her dress, a complicated tunic affair with a faint smell of mothballs, and touching up her chignon, which had been so puffed out for the occasion that it stood away from her head like a spare tire on a rumble seat. Julia in the corner was more cool and smiling than ever, but Tootsie looked as if she were sweating out a sisterhood meeting.

"So tell me," she said, sounding as if she could hardly wait to get home and take off her corselet, and also taking a quick look around to make sure Milton was no longer in earshot, "for what reason does a doll like you want to be an intellectual?"

"Intellectual?" Daisy repeated, looking past Tootsie at George Auerbach, who had now slumped in a canvas chair with a hand covering his face. "—do you mean do I want abstractions or pure idea to propel me, or intellectual in the sense of vocation? Because actually I—"

He put his hand down and their eyes met briefly.

"I mean what do you want to be like those dried-up lemons around here for? They sleep with cats. Better you should marry a professor. Then you could have all the books without the headaches, you know what I mean?"

"You remind me of my sister," Daisy murmured, smiling.

He smiled back. Excellent teeth.

"You have a sister? Funny thing, I took you for an only child."

"Well, in a way you might say I am. In a way you might even call me *sui generis*, though of course my background is ordinary middle class—"

"So what does your sister do? Also a teacher?"

"She's married. She has a baby."

"And your father?"

"Her father's a furrier," Julia said, "she has the loveliest jacket."

George Auerbach covered his face again.

"I had a mouton thing once," Tootsie said pensively, "but it was so heavy I put it in storage and left it there. Could be there still, for all I know . . ." Milton had joined George Auerbach and whispered something in his ear that made him throw back his head and laugh, and then the two of them sauntered over to the bookcase.

"What? Oh, yes, it is unusual, Mrs. Goldfarb, Tootsie, I mean, but I happened to be named after my grandmother, Dvorah Tzippah . . . Daisy starts with a D. . . ."

"Look at this, Milton," George Auerbach said, pulling out one volume after another and pushing them back in disgust. "Eliot, Donne, *The Quest for the Grail in W. H. Auden*—nothing outside of the canon, naturally. . . . Hey, Seymour, how about a little music?"

"We can't," Seymour said, picking up the little boy who had been pulling at his trouser leg. "We're going to eat in a minute. Anyhow, the hi-fi's broken again."

"I thought your father sent you the money to fix it."

"He did, but there were a few bills outstanding and Julia said—"

"Your *father*?" Daisy could not help saying. "But I thought—"

"You mean even this beautiful innocent child knows about it already?" George Auerbach asked, cocking his head at Daisy.

Seymour smiled sheepishly.

"Seymour, you're a slob."

"Right!" Seymour said, abandoning his little boy and pulling up a chair with interest.

"Forget it."

"No, really," Seymour insisted. "Go on. I want to hear what you think."

"For such news," Milton advised him, "you can wait until after dinner."

"That's right. Listen to Milton. He speaks with the wisdom of our fathers."

"Sure, it's all right for the two of you to talk," Seymour said hotly. "You both had decent fathers, whereas I—"

"Would anyone else like another drink before dinner?" Julia inquired, picking up the whisky bottle from the arms of a teddy bear where Seymour had left it.

"Oh, for Christ's sake, Julia," Seymour said testily, "stop interrupting."

"I'll bet everyone's starving," Julia remarked.

"Julia, wait a minute, dammit."

Julia waited. She also gave him one of her smiles, which though it was silent and aimed at the back of his neck was enough to make his skin turn red and his shoulders stiffen. Seymour looked around him with a crestfallen air and got to his feet. The rest of the party followed him slowly into the dining room, Daisy ducking to avoid the punching bag in the doorway, and George Auerbach narrowly avoiding the roller skate poised on the threshold.

The fancy array of dishes on the table was surprising, considering Julia's gifts for understatement: little meatballs swimming in sour cream, little mushrooms swimming in something else, trays of homemade bread and twisted rolls, rice wafting steam from a large turquoise casserole, an enormous salad bowl, all set between cracked plates of heirloom china and dented silver knives and forks. "Don't let it throw you, she got it all from Mrs. Carp's recipes," George Auerbach laughed, pulling out Daisy's chair and, as she turned to answer him, ignoring her completely. As the food passed from hand to hand, he ate like a bachelor, quickly, and with an air of sustaining life, and paused only once to gesture at Milton with a half-eaten roll and tell him he understood nothing about mathematics. "So who does understand it?" Milton said. "You?" "Of course not," George Auerbach said, "what the hell is math to me?" At the other end of the table, Julia and Tootsie were discussing Babs Pilsner whose twins had just gotten over the German measles which she claimed they had caught from Buddy Lipshansky, though as Julia pointed out this was all rather absurd since they could have gotten them anywhere. "She also claims you told her to do exercises for fucking," Tootsie said. Seymour looked up quickly, eyes shining with interest, and then with a shrug reached across Tootsie for seconds. Daisy quietly removed a paw from her neck. The other dog was slurping at her plate, and the little boy wandered by pulling shredded straw from the place mats. It was odd in a way that having spent so many hours preparing the food—or had she?—Julia hadn't taken a sponge to the table. It was still full of dried jelly spots, sticky bits of paper napkin, and also some colorful crayon work which the Lipshansky children must have been working on at breakfast time.

"This one's Seymour," George Auerbach said, tapping on a skinny stick figure in red. "You're the little writer. Why don't you write about him? The poor man's Oblomov."

"Oh?" Daisy said. "Then you do know which one I am?"

"We live in the same house, don't we?"

"Oh, yes," Daisy said, "but—"

"Besides, you're a beautiful girl. Although—" he pointed significantly to the stick Seymour, "you ought to bear one thing in mind. Meat on the bones. That's very important. Here, take some more of this. It'll build you up."

He handed Daisy the rice, watching as she plowed into it enthusiastically, like a hard-pressed Chinese. "Take it easy," he murmured with a puzzled frown. "What's the matter, did I mix you up with somebody else when you first moved in? . . . Oh, Christ, are you the one I gave my laundry to? . . . Yes, I can see you are."

Daisy shifted haughtily in her seat.

"Well, that's how it is, sweetheart," he said with a commiserating smile, "I've finally reached an age when all young girls look alike to me. And believe it or not, I prefer it that way. Less wear and tear on the intestines. Right, Milton?"

"Right," Milton sighed, shaking his head. "Although," he added, beaming suddenly, "there are cases where it might still be a pleasure to differentiate."

"You're still awake, Buddy doll?" Tootsie said quickly, clutching at the little boy who writhed away from her. "Give Tootsie a big kiss." She did not seem surprised when he immediately let out a loud wail and ran to poke his nose between his mother's breasts. The two dogs joined him at Julia's knees, followed by a kitten who scampered across the table to squint at George Auerbach passionately.

"Goddammit, Julia!" he said, throwing down his napkin in disgust. "If I wanted a zoo, I'd live in the Bronx. Every time I come here—look, take it away before it pees on my plate or something."

Julia reached across for the tiny kitten and laughed. "Oh, George, you're so sensitive. In France a thing like this wouldn't bother anybody." She cuddled it against her cheek. "Of course," she added with a sigh, "I suppose I will have to drown him someday. He was born deformed—" Julia deftly indicated a withered paw and a pink congealed eye—"but the children love him. Don't they, Seymour?"

"Yeah," Seymour said, obliviously eating away.

The sight of him appeared to remind Julia of her duties as a hostess. "Won't you all have something more?" she asked, receiving four bleak headshakes in reply. "No? What a shame. I'll get the dessert then."

It was a blanc mange and they all ate it in constrained silence, including Buddy whose nose was dripping into his, and then returned to the living room where Julia poured coffee from an elegant silver pot that gleamed with brown tarnish.

"Boy, talk about being loose," Tootsie said, heaving herself into the nearest armchair as Julia went upstairs to put Buddy to bed for the fourth or fifth time, and Seymour stayed in the kitchen having been told to see if there was any more whisky, "—what's the matter, doll, you're still nauseous?"

"I'll be all right in a minute."

"Naturally with four children it is very hard to keep clean," Tootsie added in a mincing voice, as if Daisy had just said it was easy. "You don't appreciate this because you don't have any, but let me tell you, even with one—" she laughed "—of course, my house isn't this kind of pigsty."

"Tootsie," Milton said.

"So what am I saying?" Tootsie smiled, looking more and more imprisoned in her corset. "The Lipshanskys are the salt of the earth, our best friends even, except if Seymour doesn't get tenure they'll have to leave. I tell you, doll, that's the whole trouble in a place like this. You make a friend, he's not renewed. All except Georgie there, and he's a world-famous celebrity."

"Not merely a friend, Tootsie," he corrected her, strolling from the bookcases back to the sling chair. "In Gorham you might even consider me a relative. Which reminds me," he said to Daisy, "I hear Oscar Brooks gave you a hard time the other day. Don't let it worry you. He always does it. He thinks of it as a moral duty, like a freshman initiation."

"Oh, I didn't mind it really," Daisy said. "I'm sure it hurt him more than it hurt me."

"Oh?" George Auerbach said. "Is pity your strong suit then?"

"I like to think of it more as a compassion," Daisy said, with an uneasy glance at Seymour who had just come back from the kitchen forlorn and empty-handed.

"Compassion? Have you come to weep over Gorham and save us with your tears?"

"Aw come off it," Seymour said angrily, "first you fire questions at the poor girl until she doesn't know what she's saying, and then you make fun of her."

"This one can defend herself, Seymour," George Auerbach laughed. "But let's hope you never have to find that out."

"And furthermore, there's no more whisky," Seymour retorted, loping over to the couch to give Daisy's hand a sympathetic squeeze. "Pay no attention to that bastard," he murmured. "Just because he's made a name for himself, he thinks he can go around hurting everybody's feelings."

"Actually, I was very interested in his point," Daisy said, only to have Seymour pat her hand again and assure her that he knew just how she felt. With an air of loosening his tie, although he wasn't wearing one, Seymour asked her for a cigarette, automatically explaining that he had left his pipe tobacco home, and in a few minutes was deep in a long runny chronicle about loneliness, the painful sensitivities of youth, and life on a barren New England farm. As he was about to enter Yale, he flowed away to be replaced by the powerful hum of George Auerbach's voice in the background—he was talking over his shoulder and smiling at something Julia was leaning down to tell him—strong and resonant, like an electric current. She did not understand why if people felt obliged to apologize for George Auerbach they were so eager to have him in the first place—surely it wasn't just because he was famous, or was it?—and there was no doubt that Seymour had a point about the man's manners. He acted as if his rudeness were a form of courage, and also now that she had been looking at him closely for several hours was not half so handsome as a few striking glimpses had led her to believe. He was surprisingly short, his hair was shot with gray, and his brown tweed suit had either been slept in or trampled on. Then why had she known at any precise point in the evening where George Auerbach sat and whether he was talking, or as at this moment, had fallen into one of his gloomy silences? And why did she feel sick when he patted Julia's rump familiarly, as if he had been doing it for years?

"Okay," he said, sending Julia off with a final slap and nodding in Daisy's direction. "Come on, I'll take you home."

"Take her *home*?" Seymour protested, emerging from prison camp. "It's only ten o'clock. What are you trying to do, break up the party?"

"It's all right, Seymour," Daisy said. "Really, I—"

"When she's ready to go home I'll drive her," Seymour said.

"Drive me? But I live just down the—"

"I'll take you in the car and come right back."

"Yes, do that," Julia said.

"Which one's your coat?" George Auerbach asked, ignoring them both.

"It's the fur jacket."

"Oh, yes, I forgot. Daddy's in the business."

"So what kind of fur is it?" Tootsie asked.

"Broadtail."

"You know what they tried to charge me for storage? Ten bucks a year. I nearly choked when I saw the first bill."

"Tootsie," Milton sighed.

"I'll drive her home," Seymour said doggedly.

George Auerbach exchanged a long look with Seymour over Daisy's head. "I said it was okay," he repeated, more in sorrow than in anger, and pushing Daisy into the hall, extracted her coat from the heap, sent a tired wave through to the remains of the dinner party, and shoved her out the front door.

5

IT WAS A COLD NIGHT, beautifully harvest-moonish, with a nip of frost and a touch of pumpkin in the air. Their footsteps made muffled echoes on the empty street like the faint romantic clip clop of carriage horses returning late from the ball. Shivering with the unexpected happiness of it, Daisy thrust her arm through George Auerbach's. In spite of her careful upbringing she had always loved the feel of a man close by, especially in cold weather. Unfortunately the man appeared to think otherwise, since with an odd pensive look in her direction, he carefully detached her from his sleeve like a beetle.

"Oh, well," Daisy said, "it was a nice party anyway. Or do you hate that word?"

Silence. Overhead, a full moon hinted of werewolves and possible danger.

"I suppose you've all been friends for years and years? Personally, I wasn't too keen on the dogs, but then I never do know whether it's their fault or mine. The dogs, I mean."

The answer was a puff of soundless breath condensing into white vapor in the air.

Daisy's happiness began to yield to a faint chill of the heart. It occurred to her that her knowledge of the ground rules for this sort of thing was very shaky. Perhaps a midnight walk in the country demanded the same fraught and impassioned silence as dancing. Well, no matter. The coldness of the air excited her cheeks, the man excited the rest of her. Oh, kiss me, kiss me, my exhilarating Auerbach. No? Then perhaps Elm Street would uncoil itself endlessly so that it would take them the rest of the night to get home.

"They're a bunch of hypocrites and hyenas," he said suddenly. "Academic hillbillies. How old are you, anyway?"

"Twenty-two. How old are you?"

"Don't be impertinent."

"Sorry."

"Oh, the hell with it," he said, absently putting her hand in his pocket and proceeding to walk so rapidly that Daisy, loosely attached, jogged along bumpily behind him. A few steps further on, however, his shoulders began to droop a little. He paused and gave Daisy that peculiar distracted glance of his, as if the sight of her had interrupted his thinking. Daisy smiled, a smile of the blackest despair. Her dearest wish was that he would stop making unilateral decisions. If only he—if only. . . . A short period of darkness. A blinding flash of light. A startlingly distinct impression of having been thoroughly and lewdly kissed. . . . Or had she? Her lover (?) had started down the street again, pulling her by the hand. She delicately explored her lips with the tip of her tongue. Fire. Fire and ice.

"Miss Lerner?" Once more she stopped dead in her tracks.

"Yes, sir?"

"Are you a great lover of music?"

"Passionate."

"Would you like to hear some now?"

"Oh, yes," Daisy said. "Yes, yes, yes . . . only—where will we find a concert at this hour?"

"In my apartment."

His apartment? *Ah.* For a moment, all the ugly faces of suspicion leered together. They had arrived at 69 Elm Street. Together they entered the dour old house and walked up the first flight of stairs. And then as Daisy gave a last backward glance toward her own door and lifted her chin—no, fold your wings, cold reason, sweet joy enfold us both—together they mounted the next.

"Well, how do you like it?" George Auerbach said, plucking a benzedrine inhaler from a crowded mantelpiece and explaining it as the result of a recent drafty reading at Mt. Holyoke. "The joys of country living," he said with a short bitter laugh. "I advise flannel underwear."

She tried to smile back, but with a little difficulty, since for the moment desire, pink flowers unpetaling, all seemed to have fled, and she was seeing things with the awful clarity of a girl who is about to embark on a step that will change her whole life, or with no luck not change her life at all. As he watched her over a distended nostril she glanced around at what appeared to be a storeroom of books and papers punctuated by occasional small islands of furniture. The large oval table in the center of the room was piled high under the coffee cup and bottle of Milk of Magnesia which served as paperweights, and more papers and more books were falling over each other on the Indian throw rug that covered the daybed, in addition to the piles of books and boxes of Kleenex strewn across the floor. Even the fireplace was cluttered with last Sunday's *Times* and crumpled sheets of yellow paper which had been typed on in short lines. Only the windows struck an incongruous, almost jarringly false note because somebody had hung them with curtains.

"What's the matter, are you worried because I don't have slip covers too? . . . Here, take a seat."

She was still wearing her coat. George Auerbach (no, under the circumstances oughtn't she to call him George?) had already discarded his as well as his jacket and tie, and turned on a record that was already in the phonograph.

"Where?"

"What? Oh, here." He swept off the daybed, unearthing a large bottle of bourbon. "Would you like a drink?"

"No, thank you."

"'No, thank you,'" he repeated in a mincing voice. With a shrug, he poured himself a shot and wiped his mouth with the back of his hand, looking at her closely the whole time.

"It still kills me that he's dead," Daisy said. "Doesn't it you?"

"That who's dead?"

"Mozart," she said, indicating the phonograph. "Every time I hear that quintet I have such a sense of personal loss, of youth wrenched from its—"

"No," George said.

"I beg your pardon?"

He shook his head. "Look, sweetheart, I realize you're young and you're nervous. But take my advice. Don't ever get fanciful about art, even if you're alone with a man, because art is a very serious—" he yawned and poked a finger down around the back of his collar "—listen, baby, maybe it would be better all around if you went home now. To tell you the truth, if I don't shake this cold pretty soon I won't be good for a damn thing in the morning—by which I mean my work." He paused and looked at her questioningly. "Or am I mistaken in assuming that you're familiar with it?"

"Familiar with your work?" Daisy repeated. She laughed. "Well, actually not, to be honest about it. Though what little I've read does seem to strike a chord of . . . anyhow," she added quickly, "I don't want to go home. I just got here."

"I'm thinking of your good too, believe me."

"So am I."

George smiled, rather wearily. He pulled up a chair and straddled it, looking into Daisy's face directly. "Listen, sweetheart, a few facts. I am forty-one years old. I have been legally separated, though not divorced, for five years. I have a ten-year-old son. I also write that poetry you've read a little bit of. It's my whole life, and the only thing in this world I give a damn about. As an authority on the subject, consult my wife. Ex. Almost."

"So?"

"So none of this makes you wary?"

"Why should it? Whatever you are, you are."

"I see. And do you always accept people so readily?"

"If I love them."

"And you're under the impression that you love *me*?"

"I know it. I realized it this evening."

"Don't be ridiculous."

"Excuse me," Daisy said, rather coldly. "But it's you who are being ridiculous, not to say unkind. I ought to know whether I love someone or not."

"But how could you possibly—?" he began, and when Daisy opened her mouth to interrupt, held up his hand for silence. "No, wait. This is really a hell of an argument to be having at this hour under these circumstances. I'm beginning to think your generation is even farther out than they say. Just a minute—let me turn this damn Mozart off first."

With an air of exasperation, he reached behind him to click off the phonograph, and still exasperated he caught Daisy by the back of the head and kissed her.

"Go home," he said.

"I won't."

"You're being absurd. What do you know about love, anyway? What in all your silly innocence gives you the right to lay claim to it? A tingly feeling in your groin on a warm spring day? Some romantic novel you've read? A scene from a sexy movie? A predicament you want to get out of?"

"Then give me the right," Daisy said.

"I'll impale you. You'll suffer."

"Well?"

"And you're frightened, too. I can tell."

"I'm not frightened."

"You're shivering."

"I'm cold."

"No, don't be cold," he said, "don't be cold," and caught her in his arms. As if he were hurrying to warm her, he gently stripped down the jacket, the dress, the slip, until they were all tumbled about her waist and she sat there whitely swaying, like a young ear of corn bared of its husk. ". . . oh, my god, you really are beautiful, aren't you? When you hang your head like that, you're a yellow flower . . . skinny, much too skinny . . . but so lovely."

She caught his head against her.

"I love your hair too. It's black and silver."

"Father image."

"My father is bald."

"Listen, can't you shut up?" he murmured pleadingly against her skin. "I'm trying to make love to you. . . . And you're so taut and lovely. . . . A little Etruscan statue. No, a little Renaissance Madonna." He drew back with a sudden look of horror. "My god—are you?"

"Am I what?"

"Don't play dumb."

Daisy hesitated. A hesitation so unworthy of the moment she almost wept with shame.

"Not exactly."

"What does that mean?"

"Twice before."

"Two times or two people?"

"Two people."

George laughed out loud. "Oh, my sweet lovely young Daisy," he said, pulling down the shade, and when that had tumbled to the floor, turning out the light in gentle deference to her youth.

It was still night when she tiptoed back down the stairs again, though dawn was breaking. She had never seen anything so beautiful as the gray and silver seeping beneath her doorsill or the tender looming shapes of her furniture as she glided inside. She sat down on her bed and quietly extracted a garter belt and stockings from her coat pocket, reeling and drunk with happiness, and also feeling slightly ridiculous to have put on all her clothes for one flight. But stealth was necessary, wasn't it, in a small town such as this where people pressed eyes to keyholes and peered furtively around doorways? Actually, as far as she knew the only other apartment belonged to an elderly professor of music and his wife who retired early. But George had pointed out that it was none of their business either. No, and besides, he could not ask her to spend the night with him. He had only that one single daybed and also, as he had explained kissing her good night, there was always the possibility he might be contagious. Oh, what a shame. How lovely it would have been to lie side by side, talking the night away, while their cigarette ends glowed red in the darkness. But George had stopped smoking. Another pity, she giggled to herself, more's the pity she's a . . .

With a small hiccough, she turned over the volume of his *Selected Poems* which George had given her, ("To Daisy, best from George") and sobered suddenly, remembering all the poems he had read to her tonight and the heartbreaking life story that went with them: how he had been so menaced by the philistines at such an early age, he was still haunted by the fear that they would get him: first by his mother—it did not take a trained psychiatrist to figure that out, though poor George had been to one of those too—who had kept hauling him out of his room in their Chicago tenement where he was reading his library books as she wept to heaven that he was ruining his health; and then, after her, that long line of ladies who worried terribly every time George read, or later wrote, the last of them his wife, a girl he had found literally camped on his doorstep one evening in Greenwich Village ("I hardly even knew her," he insisted. "She had bangs. I saw her once or twice necking at parties."), crying her eyes out because he was always too busy to answer the phone. The rest was now bitter history. Like a fool, George decided to meet the menace head-on, and a year later found himself wheeling a baby carriage through Central Park on the maid's day off. To make matters worse, the name of that baby, as George had revealed only an hour or two before with a terrible wrenching shudder—was Gary. *Gary*. Oh, what couldn't you *feel* for a man who told you a thing like that?

She flew to the open window, leaning out to touch the soft silent air with her face. Below, in that grove where she had once stood crying for other reasons, a quiet gray fog was seeping across the grass, rising to muffle the shapes of the foliage. A tier of ragged branches cut like a silhouette against the lightening sky. Was this a hemlock, perhaps? And beyond that, gnarled and split almost in half, a cherry tree whose white blossoms would drip to the ground in the spring? Her eye grew keener. She saw a slender pear, a tangled thicket of forsythia, masses of chrysanthemums, daffodils and roses, lilacs in profusion and all out of season. Oh, Daisy, Daisy, it's love that makes the world go round, and all of it is yours. So that she went on making up her own names for everything until, as the sky turned from pink to purple, her lilacs really did seem to be blooming.

6

"OH WELL," BABS PILSNER SAID, coming through the chill October mist to park her twins at Tootsie's house, and feeling as philosophical as she ever would. It was only nine o'clock on a Saturday morning and she had already been intercepted by Stella Brooks who had put her down for five dozen cookies for the next tea, even though she had already contributed six dozen small assorted sandwiches to the last. "Anyway, I suppose it's better than a summer sitting around in the woods trying to save your marriage. Can you imagine? There we are in this log cabin for over two months, and not once will that man lay down his thesis to discuss the matter. Honestly, Tootsie, I tell you there are times when men absolutely kill me."

Men. For a moment, yielding to the sweet subterranean memory the word itself seemed to have stirred up in her soul, Babs giggled a little and minced and batted her eyelashes as she had in Macon years ago. Then when the beau was caught, she reluctantly surrendered to her present self, a broad-beamed young matron with a straggling bun, a heavy sweater and old shirt, and a pair of Bermuda shorts which, unlike those worn by an occasional undergraduate strolling by across the street, tended to stick out in the belly.

"No, really, Tootsie," she continued as Tootsie remained standing there in the doorway, arms akimbo. "I think this week I really am going to ask Dr. Rust about those exercises Julia recommended—you know, the ones that are supposed to strengthen the muscles of the vagina."

"They definitely have exercises for that?" Tootsie said.

"Why certainly."

"*America*," Tootsie said, shaking her head and pursing her lips thoughtfully.

"Oh, honestly, Tootsie!" Babs said, as usual getting a little angry in her confusion. Now what in god's name could the United States as a country have to do with the techniques of sexual intercourse (France, yes, China maybe, if you wanted to be obscene), and beyond that why was Tootsie always trying to deflect her from the heart of a perfectly fascinating subject? Jews, she thought to herself, knowing that Bill would disapprove, but feeling perverse enough to risk it—they were certainly the trickiest, most misleading people in the world, to say the least. Why, to this day, even after two years of knowing better, the sight of Tootsie with those big breasts and gold back teeth could still deceive her into thinking that anyone could run to Tootsie with their troubles and practically be smothered with comfort. Whereas, as Babs knew from very sad experience, practically the opposite was true. Tootsie was perfectly capable of advising you that an old diaphragm made an excellent teething ring for a baby, and letting it go at that. And the odd part was that it never seemed to occur to Tootsie how *liberal*-minded Babs was to come to Tootsie Goldfarb with her troubles in the first place. She looked worriedly at the twins beating each other with shovels on the weedy steps, remembering that she was due to take Tootsie's baby on Thursday and on Saturday all of Julia's.

"How's Milton's schedule this term, by the way?" she asked.

"The same lousy fifteen hours," Tootsie said. "Bill has more?"

"A little," Babs said reluctantly. ". . . Oh, shit on wheels! I think we just spoil these men worrying about them so much. What's so tough about shooting your mouth off and reading a few books anyway? If you ask me, being a full-time mother is a lot harder than teaching and just as creative." The day seemed to be freshening up. Down the street, Seymour Lipshansky had come out to lean his rake on a pile of dead leaves, and eye a girl or two who dribbled out of the dormitory yawning and stretching. "Of course," Babs giggled, "in Seymour's case maybe it's a lucky thing they work him so hard. Maybe it'll keep him out of trouble for a while."

"What trouble?" Tootsie said.

"*What* trouble?" Babs repeated, giggling a little harder out of a sudden fear that she had said the wrong thing. "Well, I mean, everyone knows, don't they . . . ?" She looked to Tootsie for help, dimly remembering that it was Tootsie who had told her the story in the first place, and under Tootsie's Buddha-like look of disdain, the rest of her sentence ended itself in a short choked gurgle.

"Oh, well," Babs said, by now laughing helplessly. "It doesn't matter anyway. I mean, it does matter but—" Seymour was no longer looking at the girls. He was watching George Auerbach hurry down the street with his jacket collar turned up and his hands shoved deep in his pockets. Another one of *them*, Babs thought, always saying what he pleased even if it was nasty and leering, always feeling free to take the law into his own hands, so to speak. Of course, Bill admired his work very much. Bill said he was one of the best poets of his generation. Which still didn't give him the right to—"Hello, Georgie," Tootsie said glumly. ". . . Good morning, ladies. . . ." Tootsie swiveled her head to follow George as he disappeared into the dark covered porch of 69 Elm Street, and Babs swiveled hers too, waiting intently a few moments after the door had banged behind him before she raised her eyes to the third floor, and then (still following Tootsie's lead), back down one. For a few moments the two women continued to stare upwards until, still locked in that thoughtful camaraderie, they turned towards each other. Babs reached into her buxom pocket for a cigarette. On days like this, Babs thought, sitting down on Tootsie's damp porch step with a thump, she could not help feeling that life had played some practical joke on her, which being good-natured Babs would not have minded so much if life would only stop sometimes and explain what the joke was.

"Really?" Stella Brooks asked, laughing nervously and brushing a few dry leaves from her person as her husband poured out the sherry by their hearthside. "Well, does this mean that when we have George to dinner, which I'm afraid we must sooner or later, we also—?"

"Now, now, my dear," Professor Brooks smiled, twirling an amber glass to which Stella shook her head as she stowed away her binoculars, and then offering it to their guest, Dr. William Rust, the college physician, who leaned forward to accept in a brief flicker of firelight. "We obviously can't do without a Poet-in-Residence. But as to the rest of it, well why not let's wait and see?"

As he neatly fitted the stopple back into the neck of the decanter he exchanged a glance with Dr. Rust, who thoughtfully took a sip of his drink and then puffed at his pipe and succeeded in looking, on account of his prematurely white hair and handsome hound's tooth jacket (and possibly because he happened to be fingering a volume of W. Somerset Maugham just at that moment), as if he were the friend and confidant of most of the families of Gorham, which alas, he was not, and also (suddenly Professor Brooks hoped heartily that it was not George Auerbach who had made this observation) as if a German shepherd dog were perpetually missing from his side, which in fact it was. The dog was home with Dr. Rust's wife and five children, each of whom played a different musical instrument. But of course a man could be perfectly devoted to his family and music and animals and still seek out old friends in the interests of other aspects of culture, a habit that Dr. Rust had been pursuing with Stella and Oscar Brooks for almost twenty years now.

"Brunch?" Dr. Rust repeated, diffidently removing his pipe and smiling as if he had not received the same invitation under the same circumstances the previous Saturday. "—why, yes, certainly, I'd be very happy to stay, Stella, if you're quite sure that it won't be too much trouble."

"Now how can there be trouble between old friends and fellow bird watchers?" Stella Brooks laughed, making her customary response but with a perceptible crack in her usual gay façade. And before Dr. Rust could do more than faintly lift his eyebrows, strode off to the kitchen where the maid had already started on the eggs, though naturally with her love of informality, Stella never let Mrs. Baines wait on table.

"Perhaps, after all," Dr. Rust began, "I—"

"Nonsense, William," Professor Brooks said. "Stella is probably just a bit preoccupied with her next tea. You know how Stella is about her teas."

"She gives herself so," Dr. Rust agreed, sounding somewhat, though not altogether reassured. "And I suppose I shouldn't have brought up this recent, unfortunate mockery of our liberal policy. Still, I don't see how even Stella in all her innocence could have missed it for long. Arm in arm down Elm Street every morning, the pair of them, passionate discussions right in the middle of campus, nudging and whispering so much at Rosemary Hall last night I could hardly catch a word of the rebuttal. Frankly, I'm amazed that a person of George Auerbach's intellectual caliber would stoop to—"

"Very talky lovers, apparently," Professor Brooks said with an air of sophisticated amusement. "Oh, come now, William, let's not exaggerate. What is it, after all, but something which from a literary point of view we all ought to have been expecting anyway in the year of the *Selected Poems*? Personally, I haven't the slightest doubt that George will come to his senses very soon and realize he's only making a fool of himself."

"Yes, but what about the girl, Oscar?"

"As for the young lady," Professor Brooks shrugged and smiled, "though I confess to a disappointment that her ambitions appear to be of a less 'delicate' nature, shall we say, than I would have expected from certain conversations . . ." A beautiful cloud of colored butterflies unexpectedly fluttered through his mind ". . . not that she isn't quite sweet, really, and surprisingly successful with her students. At least, they seem to find her amusing—"

"I'm sure they do," Dr. Rust said.

"Yes," Professor Brooks said, shaking his head to clear it and then bringing himself firmly back to the present with a cough "—yes, well as I was about to say, so long as she performs her duties adequately— and I assure you I made it perfectly clear at Friday's meeting that by November first we are all to be out of the periodic sentence and well into the paragraph—and so long as—"

"Yes, yes," Dr. Rust interrupted, "but departmental questions aside, Oscar, isn't there another point at issue here?"

"I beg your pardon?"

"Since, after all, isn't what concerns us, or ought to, that this little fling has been going on in *Gorham* for the past week or two?"

"Well, yes," Professor Brooks said with a tinge of reluctance, "to a limited degree I'd be inclined to—"

"I don't think you realize what an unhealthy emotional climate will be built up here if this sort of thing continues," Dr. Rust said, taking another puff or two of his pipe before he underscored his next remarks with it. "George is a local hero. The young woman is a vivid blonde of the kind that, let's be frank about it, a town like Gorham doesn't specialize in. It's a time of year when our girls ought to be looking towards midterms. Instead of which, what will be happening? Up until midnight with their fantasies, gorging themselves out of cracker boxes and pickle jars. If it can happen to her, why not to them? And then in the morning the poor things will come staggering down to me in the Infirmary with their dark circles and new pimples, some of them probably even feverish."

"Yes, but strictly *entre nous*, let's be honest," Professor Brooks smiled, "they're of an age, our girls, aren't they, when they always do go to bed burning with lust?"

"And are supposed," Dr. Rust answered wryly, "to wake up unextinguished."

As he reached for the decanter again, Oscar Brooks glanced around with a strong personal sense of satisfaction, almost as if he could see a group of the younger faculty listening to this conversation he and William were having. For of course, far from being stodgy—yes, he knew perfectly well what people like young Lipshansky said about him—he and Stella and their friends were actually very advanced, but in private where it really counted. Witness this sherry before brunch, witness their voting for Adlai Stevenson both in 1952 and 1956. Witness above all this house itself, by far the most modernistic one in Gorham, which they had built by hiring an assistant to one of the country's foremost architects, and even consenting to shut themselves away at the Inn while the young man hacked away at a slant on a hillside and refused to answer the phone when they called. Once, about ten years ago, as Oscar Brooks seemed to remember it, there was an aspiring young assistant professor who had tried to imitate the result, but with such pale success (or had he left for other reasons?) that ever since then this house had remained the unchallenged, even one might say, the Ur version. It was all on one level, and everything in it was absolutely functional (except for the bedroom door that Stella in a sudden access of Victorianism had caused to be put up secretly and at extra expense). Cupboards, square chairs, tables, all jutted sideways and immovable from the walls, and in the living room the striking effect came from this enormous rising red brick hearth which was always kept lit so that on a cold morning like this when the light died in the north, everything was wrapped in an unusual incandescent gloom. He had always been proud of this gloom, Stella also; he considered it extremely meditative, and if sometimes it was the slightest bit reminiscent of Beowulf, well that was fitting too, wasn't it, because of course Oscar Brooks *was* a specialist in Early English.

"Mumbo jumbo, mumbo jumbo," Dr. Rust remarked, as Professor Brooks nodded contentedly.

"Excuse me?" Stella Brooks said, returning with two pitchers and proceeding to fill the long-stemmed goblets on the table with water for William, and milk for herself and her husband.

"Your speech, for the Amelia Lacey Memorial Ceremony," Dr. Rust said, "I was just wondering if you'd written it yet."

"Goodness no!" Stella Brooks exclaimed. "How could I? It's weeks and weeks away still, and with all these other demands on me—" She broke off, obviously fearing that she had sounded a bit too shrill. "In any case, William," she said, attempting a more gracious note, "inspiration still fails. Perhaps the muses will speak before the event."

"They always have, my dear," Dr. Rust said, "and very eloquently too, if I may say so. As a poor mundane medical man, I always look forward to the charming picture you make standing by the grave with the wreath in your hand."

"Last year it was raining," Stella Brooks said. "I thought it was so lovely and appropriate."

"Then perhaps," Professor Brooks smiled to Dr. Rust as William more or less ladled Stella into her place (the chair was bolted to the floor and did not pull out), "perhaps, my dear, the weather will be bad again this year."

Outside of Daisy's window, a little bird hopped from branch to branch of the hemlock tree, twittering and cheeping and making all the other small sounds of life. She opened her eyes.

"Good morning, my darling," Daisy murmured contentedly, squirming out of drowsy sheets to hold out her arms. "What time is it, anyway, have you any idea?"

"Later than you think," George said, who had been standing beside her bed, muttering as he looked down on her, this morning something about "a little pearly Venus yawning on her half shell," and then "the hell with it," and—shrugging and unzipping his trousers—could she kindly move over? He glanced grimly toward the window and climbed in beside her, in his shorts but still wearing his white shirt and brown rep tie, so that he looked curiously formally dressed for the occasion, as if from the top up he were about to give her a reading. "You were asleep again," he added, almost as if she had not realized it.

"Profound emotion always conks me out," Daisy said, quickly scooping up several of the freshman bluebooks that were scattered across her blanket. "I think it's because subconsciously I'm terrified of reaching its outer limits." And when George made a noise, smiled and touched his cold cheek with faintly guilty fingertips. ". . . whereas you are all clean and bright and shiny and smooth-shaven and have already put in several hours at the library, all before breakfast. Am I right?"

"I told you," George said. "It's nothing to envy, only a form of insomnia. My whole life I've been walking around getting my best ideas on an empty stomach."

"And then you come to me with great tidings of the outside world. Oh, I love that."

"I can't vouch for the great outside world, sweetheart," George said, poking a thumb toward the tree-scraped window. "But if you're interested in what goes on in this town, I can assure you there isn't anybody from the lowliest freshman to your pal Seymour—if that's an ascending scale—who isn't talking and worrying about what we're doing in bed right this minute."

"And do you mind being notorious?" Daisy said, as a faint blush rose to her cheeks in spite of herself.

"Look, Daisy," George said gently, "for myself I've nothing to lose. You know that. I just hope you're not taking all this too seriously, that's all. I'd hate to think that just because we've happened to make love a few times—"

"A few times!"

"—or that I've privately read you a few of my unpublished poems and publicly been seen holding your hand at a symposium that it's a proposal of marriage, or anything like that, because I'm afraid, as anyone out there can tell you—"

"Marriage?" Daisy said. "Isn't it awfully early for us to be thinking about marriage?"

"Oh?" George said, turning his head towards her. "Well, aren't we the little bourgeoise."

"I thought I was being bohemian," Daisy said, passionately wrapping her legs around his, which were hard and hairy. "—oh god, you've no idea how I miss you at night. This bed is terribly grudging. And actually I never mind catching anything."

"I suppose," George said, "you think you're too young to marry?"

"Well, naturally, there are all those things I want to do first."

"Such as?"

"Oh, you know—the usual. What we were talking about yesterday in the faculty club. Bare my breast to destiny. Write."

"I wish you wouldn't talk about writing as airily as you talk about love," George said. "At least where people can hear you."

"I never talk about love airily with you," Daisy said in a hurt voice. "How could I?"

"Oh, Daisy," George sighed, "you're really still a child. You haven't a clue yet what it means to be a writer. You haven't the slightest idea what you have to sacrifice to be one."

"I'd sacrifice *everything*."

"Including me?"

"Oh, my god," Daisy said, suddenly stunned. "I never thought about that."

"Then go on," George laughed, "think about it now."

"But why would I have to give you up, who would ever, I mean—?" She sat up. "Oh, George! A goose just walked over my grave. *Please, please* hold me close."

"If you'd stop leaping off precipices before you get to the edge, idiot," George murmured into her hair, "you wouldn't fall on your face so often. I was only teasing you." He kissed her. "And by the way," George said, with his lips against her temple, "you never did tell me— who the hell were the two other ones?"

"They wouldn't interest you," Daisy said, cuddling closer. "They're not the kind of people you'd want to meet."

"I didn't say I wanted to meet them."

"But what difference do they make? . . . All right, the first one was queer. I was trying to cure him."

"They're incurable."

"Yes, and then he wanted to marry me, and I thought, but now I'll have to *talk* to him the rest of my life and—darling, isn't this obscene?"

"Number two?"

"I don't care about him. My life is full of you now. You don't care about him either."

"As a matter of fact, I don't. But how do you know that?"

"Because I love you," Daisy said. "Why do you never believe me?"

"Oh damn you, Daisy," George said. "I was minding my own business. Who the hell asked you to pick on *me?*" and got out of bed to pull down the shade. Then with a strange fearful shudder, he sank into her arms and made love to her at last.

. . . he had finally dozed off, her darling, Daisy thought, wondering why he always fought so hard each time; he had finally dozed off with his head in her neck, as if he trusted her to lead him back to the library. She put her arms around him and closed her eyes against the top of his head and tried to sleep too, pretending that the bed was a raft and that it was carrying them both safely off to sea. But it was so hard to ignore the shore. The room was growing brighter and brighter with sunshine. It was turning out to be a beautiful day. Could they be true, all those terrible things George was always telling her about everyone outside, particularly the Lipshanskys, whom he seemed to despise the most? A fact of which poor Seymour was evidently aware, since he kept looking at her reproachfully every time she passed the window of the coffee shop, as if she were a candle and he were a singed moth. And did Stella Brooks really make a practice of nabbing every newcomer for a speech the minute they hit town? George said that no one even remembered any longer who had elected Stella Brooks president of the Ladies of Gorham in the first place, and that if she ever tried to operate that organization of hers on a national scale, the ACLU would make a test case out of her. But of course it was natural that with his tragic background, he should be suspicious of everything. She propped herself up on her elbow to look at him, watching over her love in broad daylight as she had longed to do at night—oh, how fretfully he slept—and touched his handsome face with her fingertip on the vulnerable places between his brows and the edges of his mouth, tracing the little lines and scars of all his private wars, torn between pity for his exhaustion and an almost aching pride that he had spent himself on her.

"I'm an old man," George murmured. "How about some breakfast instead?"

Breakfast? Somehow she had not realized that food (and also drink) would be quite so important in this situation. And besides, what was there in the house that had not been ravaged, so to speak, by passion?

"Oh, please be happy," Daisy whispered entreatingly. "Please be happy together. I have three oranges in the ice box. We could take them and juggle for Our Lady."

Shaking his head, George reached for her hand, and then the two of them lay there for a while in silence, warmed by the sunshine that had flooded the whole room.

"*Beauty and innocence sweetly entwine/Tender and leafy their me and their thine . . .*" George turned his moist green eyes on her. "Do you know it? It's by my friend, Bill Atkinson."

"Oh, yes, he's the one whose notice we were looking at in the library."

"Listen, whom *have* you read?" George laughed.

"How do you mean that, darling, for courses or on my own?"

"I just meant who are your favorite writers? You never seem to refer to any somehow."

"Yes, I do. Let's see now. Didn't I mention Dickens our first night. My god was that only—?"

"But which poets? Whitman?"

"No," Daisy said, "not particularly."

"You might be interested in his prose."

"I didn't know he wrote any."

"What about D. H. Lawrence?"

"You mean his prose?"

"I mean his poetry."

Daisy cleared her throat. "I don't know that very well either."

There was a pause, a very long pause during which Daisy's raft teetered and tossed on a choppy sea.

"Tell me," George said at last, "do you really think it's possible even for a blonde to write books without having read any?"

The raft had split into two distinct halves. Inexorably they were drifting away from each other, growing smaller and smaller.

"I suppose I hurt your feelings just now?" George said. "Did I? Well, goddammit, stop crying and answer me."

"It's *love* that makes the world go round!" Daisy wept. "It *has* to be!"

"Warmed-over Edgar Guest," George snapped, hastily wiping his own eyes with a corner of the pillowcase. "No, it doesn't."

"Oh, my darling, I know what's bothering you. I really do. But it's not our fault, we can't help it if we're not star-crossed."

George gave her a long deep look, brimming over with utter tenderness and the darkest gloom. As he laid her to rest against his shoulder, she could feel him gazing off over her head.

7

THE ROOMS OF PRESIDENT STEEL'S LOVELY MANSION were filling rapidly. Every few moments the door under the amber fanlight
opened and closed and more ladies deposited their coats to join with
the others already milling around under the white spiral staircase or
standing beneath the large heavy portraits of former presidents and
little girls with sashes, daughters of the Kingsley family who had origi-
nally owned this house. There were stout ladies and meager ladies,
hatted ladies with stiff veils or little spear-like victorious feathers,
ladies in loose printed silk dresses, or in knitted suits stretched over
the sensible armor of their corsets. In and out among them, hostesses
wove with silver platters, so that nervous as she was about things to
come—yes, Oscar was right when he said that these teas were always
a drain on her energies (though today for reasons she had wished to
spare him)—Stella Brooks could hardly deny to herself that so far
everything was proceeding splendidly.

She passed on into the drawing room, always her favorite, perhaps
because she could so easily imagine Amelia Lacey flitting down to it
from her cupola long before President Steel was President Steel but
when Gorham was already firmly Gorham, and where amid much

chatting and the tinkle of quiet laughter, another group of ladies clustered together, carrying teacups from one occasional table to the next, or bending over one delicate sofa or another: the hard core of all her tea parties, people who had been here as long as she and Oscar. "Why, hello, there, how good of you to come. . . . Ah, Mrs. Lord, so delightful to see you here, as always," Stella Brooks murmured, ". . . and Mrs. Dimanche, so self-effacing I barely noticed you. Can I tempt you with one of these?"

"No, thank you, ma'am," Mrs. Dimanche drawled, wearing steel-rimmed magnifying glasses and a beret fastened to her front with a large hat pin. "I've already had an elegant sufficiency."

Uncertain whether to laugh, Mrs. Brooks settled for a smile (it was almost impossible to tell when a Southern lady was being funny), and turned reluctantly towards that other, rigid rim lined up against the wall, the ladies in black with rhinestone buckles, who came to every tea, sat themselves down on the edge of the settees with their galoshes planted right on the designs in the Persian carpets, refused anything to eat or drink, and rose in a body when the party was over as if a bell had rung and released them simultaneously. "Really?" Stella Brooks insisted gently, . . . "not even a drop?" turning from a gnarled New England native to a plump Pole from one of the outlying tobacco farms to a swarthy and suspicious Italian, and reminded herself as she straightened up, that no matter what people like George Auerbach said, it was not so easy to be the president of an organization—"our democratic organization," she hastily amended—so democratic that it even included wives of Maintenance.

Not, god knew, Stella Brooks thought, continuing on towards the dining room, that it was the actual work which had fallen on her shoulders that ever bothered her. ("Your too-slender shoulders," Oscar Brooks often said, forgetting, dear man, that she was five feet ten in her stocking feet.) Why, for years friends like Sue Carp had always remarked on her cheerfulness in taking on the trying business of mailing hundreds of mimeographed postcards, and enlisting hostesses, and directing heart-shaped watercress sandwiches to their proper platters, and selecting chairladies for the special events like the Annual Faculty Picnic, or the Arbor Day Festival, or the Greek

Games (though not, of course, for the Amelia Lacey Memorial Ceremony). No, there was only one aspect of it all that ever chilled her
spirits, today to the freezing point—the need each year to call on
some member of the faculty to give a talk for her ladies that would be
"both interesting and also educational." Unfortunately, she seemed to
have exhausted the older members years ago, literally—one of them,
Professor Simpson of philosophy, had pleaded laryngitis so many
times he now merely pointed mutely to his plaid muffler whenever
their cars passed in the street. And as for these newcomers, they
were always willing, of course—how could they not be?—but also
so passionate about their subjects, there was simply no telling in
advance how far their ardor was likely to take them. As for example
that young adenoidal Slavic specialist, who had read to them from
the works of Mayakovsky last year for two solid hours in Russian,
claiming that the poems were untranslatable, while the younger
women who were paying for baby sitters sat trapped on the edges of
their chairs, like fugitives in a sudden Siberian blizzard. Or—even
now Stella Brooks shuddered to think of it—the year before that
when the bearded young person from the art department had lugged
in that enormous painting of an abstract woman with those astonishing mammary glands—not to mention pubic hair (Stella Brooks'
eyes squeezed shut)—and proceeded to go at it with a pointer, ticking off so exactly how form followed function that there could never
be any doubt about it again. The painting was called Earth Mother.
(Or was it Mother Earth?) Or, in many ways worse still, that incredibly spirited exegesis of "The Miller's Tale" from the aspiring Chau-
cer specialist (no longer aspiring), which, coming from a dull young
man with rimless eyeglasses ...

But why torture herself further? When the others spoke Stella
Brooks had merely felt herself to be teetering on the edge of an abyss.
Today she could almost feel the cold air rushing about her plummet-
ing body. Why, why, why, she asked herself despairingly, had she ever
yielded to expediency and asked that girl to speak? And what, in spite
of years of experience—and with that uncanny resemblance staring
her right in the face!—had ever possessed her to suggest the topic herself? *Problems of the Creative Woman.* The pitfalls of that particular

subject in the mouth of today's particular speaker suddenly began to suggest themselves to her so alarmingly, bouncing off her mind like ping-pong balls—"unfettered self-expression," "single standard," "poetic license"—that she swayed a little on her feet, even though they were clad in her sensible bird-watching shoes.

An empty silver platter recalled her to her sense of duty. Removing it from Mrs. Pilsner's outstretched hands and redirecting her to the coffee cups, Stella Brooks entered the dining room and with a sense of relief turned to greet her friend, Mrs. Carp.

"Hello, Sue dear, can I tempt you with—oh. . . ."

Mrs. Carp looked up from a saucer lined with tea sandwiches, all of which she had bitten into speculatively. "Stella, *ma chère*," she said with a full mouth, "the pink ones are marvelous. What's in them?"

"I couldn't say, dear," Stella Brooks said distractedly, "you'll have to ask Mrs. Lipshansky. She made them."

"Lipshansky? Is that Housing and Grounds?"

"No, an alumna actually, the wife of one of our young instructors, a Clark on her side, I believe."

"Ah, that explains it," Mrs. Carp said, nodding with Stella at shy Mrs. Steel who had understood from the start that merely being the President's wife did not give her entrée into all circles, and who was quietly pouring out tea at a large table full of damask and heavy silver. Across from her, Mrs. Sylvia Sovereign, the relict of an earlier, sterner president, presided at the coffee urn, looking curiously like a photograph Stella Brooks had once seen of a Russian soldier crossing a bridge, perhaps because she was wearing two watches, one on each wrist. The rest of the women in the room were still young, newly hatched Ladies of Gorham, most of them hatless and over made-up like Mrs. Pilsner, but trying in their fledgling fashion to do their best for their husbands. Which, though commendable, was no inducement to linger, since there was no way of telling yet who of them would be asked to stay on. Very reluctantly, Stella Brooks put down her silver platter on the Sheraton sideboard, girding herself for the moment she had been dreading. Had the speaker arrived on time, at least? Yes, there she was, talking in the foyer with Mrs. Goldfarb (naturally) who looked under the amber fanlight like a fossil fly trapped in some sticky liquid. But the other one, the girl, was practically bathing in that golden glow, hair and eyes light and shining, smiling radiantly all around her. If one could only slap a tissue paper over her—a perfect frontispiece.

"But to be so brazen, so *en plein soleil!*" Sue Carp murmured, arresting a tiny sandwich between mouth and platter. Stella Brooks looked back toward the drawing room where her beloved hard core milled about in the beautiful cold north light coming from the French windows and felt more than ever that she was about to betray them.

"*Gesheft?*" Tootsie Goldfarb repeated, smiling around Daisy and over Daisy's head as if she expected somebody to come and catch her doing something dirty. "You want to know how's *gesheft?*"

She was wearing another one of her company get-ups, this time a suit that had clearly ridden out the depression, not without suffering, and was made of some dark historic material—bombazine? bengaline?—with a long row of buttons that started somewhere between Tootsie's chubby calves, and worked their way over her stomach up to her neck where they threatened to choke her.

"And, oh, look," Daisy continued, clutching at Tootsie's arm, which stiffened instantly "—there's Julia. And Babs too. My god, I never dreamed so many people would come to hear me. I'm getting scared to death suddenly."

"Don't worry too much," Tootsie advised her, strangling out a laugh. "They didn't just come to hear you. They come to hear anybody."

"Really? But why would everyone—?"

"If you're a wife, she sends you a postal card. Free will doesn't concern her."

"Yes, I know, George told me about that. But that still doesn't mean you have to—"

"Maybe you'll tell George I have a husband named Milton," Tootsie smiled, "maybe you'll explain to George, doll, that this means I *do* have to. Yes, doll?"

"Oh, but, Tootsie, please don't think that I—"

"Here you are, Tootsie," Babs Pilsner said, coming through the group sideways with a cup of coffee in her hand. "Three sugars, and heavy on the cream, that's what you said, wasn't it? . . . Oh, why, hello there."

"Hi, Babs."

"Oh, and by the way," Babs added to Tootsie with a pointedly cool smile, "have I told you that I've been rereading *Anna Karenina* lately, and that I think she was a very childish person?"

Was this a piece of news Tootsie had been waiting to hear? Suddenly, after an even deeper drop into misery, her face lit up with a bright juicy smile that went wafting far past Daisy's left shoulder, accompanied by a cheery wave from Tootsie's plump little hand. Daisy turned to see Stella Brooks flutter a greeting back and prepare to advance on them.

"Yeah, well so long, doll," Tootsie said, handing her cup back to Babs. "I'm running now. Enjoy."

"But didn't you say just now—" Daisy began.

"She saw me, doll, she saw me," Tootsie explained impatiently, edging away. She dived into a group of tinkling ladies, with Babs Pilsner and the coffee cup right behind her.

". . . Well, there you are!" Mrs. Brooks said. "And right on time too!" With a practiced glance she indicated that Julia Lipshansky, who was approaching with a tray of tea sandwiches, should take it elsewhere. ". . . Not that anyone said you were going to be late, of course," Mrs. Brooks added with a whinnying little laugh. "It's just that one is accustomed to allow literary personalities a little more—what *is* the word I'm looking for?—than one allows oneself."

"Latitude?" Daisy suggested absently, as she watched Julia carry the trayful of food farther and farther away.

"Latitude," Mrs. Brooks repeated in a rather hollow voice.

"Not that I include *us* in the category, of course," Daisy laughed, continuing to shake the moist hand that had been presented to her until it slowly slid away, "what I meant was—"

"Actually," Mrs. Brooks said, managing to eke out a smile, "I do happen to have a few literary inclinations of my own. Only in the most modest sense, of course."

"Oh, yes," Daisy said. "I remember now that—"

"A few little verses scribbled when I can. A small watercolor on a facing page."

"Watercolors, too. Oh my."

"—and perhaps if I didn't have such a strong sense of my *social* responsibilities—"

"Have you tried getting out of them?" Daisy suggested, almost a last resort. "Have you tried being firm?"

Mrs. Brooks looked bleakly off into the dining room. "I seem to see that the hostesses are already beginning to set up the folding chairs," she sighed, "so perhaps it would be best to proceed. . . . Incidentally, I don't suppose you've changed your mind about the topic? It was only a suggestion, as I tried to make clear, the merest suggestion."

"And I can assure you," Daisy said, drawing herself up and trying to make up in dignity what Mrs. Brooks made her feel she lacked in height, "that I've put my heart into it."

"Have you?" Mrs. Brooks murmured faintly, ". . . how kind. . . . But perhaps you'll want to bear in mind that not all of our membership may be as *intense* on the subject as you are . . . ," and taking Daisy by the hand began to thread her through the assembled ladies with a murmured "do pardon us, won't you?" and a "why, how perfectly wonderful to see you here," and a deft little push here and there until she finally deposited her on the window seat like a matter that would have to be dealt with later.

Intense, Daisy repeated to herself thoughtfully, sliding her notes out of their manila folder. There was something about the word "intense" that made it follow her and George around town like a puppy dog. Even Julia Lipshansky used it in her own cool way, particularly when she inquired about George's health, which she did surprisingly often, laughing with the same fastidious amusement as when she took her children feverish and runny-nosed to see Dr. Rust. It was Julia too who had told her about the hockey rink that Edgar Dudley flooded and froze for skating each winter and suggested that the fun and fresh air might do George a world of good. Not that George would take kindly to such an idea, coming from Julia; George would never take kindly to anything from the Lipshanskys (oddly enough, in fact, his favorite relaxation was to drop in on Tootsie and Milton and watch a little TV with his belt unbuckled)—but the truth was, though this was hardly the moment to dwell on it, that, well, happiness was not doing as much for George as she had hoped. He was simply not flourishing under it. Of course, so little time had passed, not much more than a month, and yet he had gone off to his latest reading at Williams looking distinctly miserable, and returned muttering things about the dignity of man, and rummaging in his closet for his vaporizer.

As Stella Brooks continued to address herself to the gathering, informing them of the dates of future meetings, which it was mandatory to attend, and how much cash had been raised by the pie sale, Daisy reminded herself to run through her notes. Not that she thought her little talk would move mountains ("Only a little thing of ten minutes or so, of practically no consequence," she had laughed to George when he asked her from the typewriter where the hell she was going all dressed up), and as Tootsie had made painfully clear, no one was going to listen anyway, but suddenly her heart began to race, and she fingered the pearls on her black dress asking herself if she had spent enough time rehearsing and making faces at herself in the bathroom mirror. Because wasn't it possible, captive audience though they were, and whether they realized it or not, that there was one subject on which she was becoming something of an expert and on which she really could inform Stella's Ladies? And couldn't this be the moment to reach out to them, hold out her arms (figuratively speaking, of course) and—she referred back to her notes again, raising her eyebrows with a flare of pleasure and flipping to the next page with a sudden feverish interest. Yes, there it was, that vital point on the word "creative" and how it was so often foolishly squandered on every meaningless, trifling human activity, "whereas. . . ." Over at the lectern Mrs. Brooks was still plodding through her introduction, which Daisy had not been listening to, except to look up every time her name was mentioned.

"—and in addition, Miss Lerner is *presently* a member of our department of English. Her topic for today is one she tells me is very close to her heart and on which she will offer us a few random comments. She has assured me that she will be brief and I know that you in return will give her your most courteous attention. And now—without further ado—Miss Daisy Lerner."

Daisy shot up.

". . . Mrs. Brooks! . . . Ladies! . . ."

At the word "Gentlemen!" Mrs. Brooks leaned forward, made a face like a strangled fish, and subsided. But none of the audience was looking at Mrs. Brooks any longer except an old lady with a hearing aid. They were all staring at Daisy, which had the unfortunate effect, like the sun's rays pinpointed through a magnifying glass, of generating a great deal of heat. As the minutes went on, she tried to remember to smile as she spoke, smiling harder when she realized that in her enthusiasm for the topic she had gone without lunch (just a quick rummage through the chirping refrigerator), and that the hostesses had kept carrying the canapés off to other parts of the party. The result was making itself audible, a kind of intestinal bass counterpoint to her main theme. Somebody's hand (Julia Lipshansky's?) thrust a glass of water under her nose. She took a gingerly sip, half expecting to erupt. But to her surprise, the boiling and grumbling sputtered out, and no one seemed to have noticed it, except possibly Mrs. Brooks who had materialized at her elbow in an unexpected show of solidarity. With a nod and a sideways smile, Daisy gathered herself up for the first of several crescendos.

"And so, let us remember, in speaking of our word 'creative' that it must be used sparingly. Not on those among us plying humdrum tasks. Not at all. We must treasure it for the *real* artist in his utter, painful isolation. For the one who, back to the horizon, lifts his voice and—"

She herself stepped backwards, gripped by an emphatic hand.

"Thank you! Thank you!" Stella Brooks exclaimed, replacing her at the lectern with astonishing speed. ". . . And now ladies, I just want to remind you again that our next meeting will take place two weeks from today. And after that the final major event sponsored by our organization this semester will be the Amelia Lacey Memorial Ceremony, which as we all know—"

". . . lifts his (or her) voice and. . . ."

Mrs. Brooks glanced at her speaker, then at her audience, and back at her speaker again. "And please remember, my friends," she said pleadingly, "coincidental appearances notwithstanding—that our own

Amelia Lacey wrote poems no one even knew about until after she was dead."

She sank back on the window seat, pulling Daisy with her, while the Ladies and, after a moment, Daisy too, joined her in fervent applause.

"But what does she always have to stick around *me* for?" Tootsie said, as Milton went on frowning at the large pile of blue examination booklets on the dining room table. "There aren't any other homes? There aren't any other people? And then in addition, must she always . . . ?"

She sighed sullenly as Milton disentangled the hand that was mixed up in his hair. "What's the matter, Miltie, you're nervous?"

"I'm not nervous."

"It's all those tests they make you mark. They work you too hard."

"How was the speech?" Milton asked.

"How should I know?" Tootsie said. "Do I ever stay for them?" and decided to go check on the baby again.

He was still fast asleep, just as Tootsie had left him in her darkened bedroom—yes, she knew Dr. Spock disapproved of his being there, but she could not help defying him on this one point—all nicely curled up in his crib and looking even fatter than he did in the morning because his cheeks had gone loose and were lolling over his face. Tootsie leaned over the bars to give him a long moist kiss, brushed some dried pablum off his forehead, and went into the bathroom where she put on the light and absently inspected a dead front tooth that was turning black. Then she sucked out a piece of the round steak they had had for lunch and put out the light again, feeling slightly at odds with herself, as she often did on tea party days. It was still early, only four o'clock. The dishes from one meal had been washed and dripped themselves dry in the drain-board, it was too soon to start thinking about the next, and there was still a good hour to go before she could decently turn on the television set, though why it should be all right for George Auerbach to watch television in the afternoon if he wanted to and somehow corrupt for other people, she did not altogether understand. Not that Tootsie questioned Milton's feelings about these matters. Unlike some other faculty wives she could mention who were always pushing themselves where they did not belong, including the ones who did those crappy ceramic ashtrays, Tootsie was perfectly happy to have Milton make the intellectual decisions in the family. And at that she considered herself fortunate to be able to sit around in front of the set for a few hours each evening without feeling too ashamed of herself, culturally speaking. In some homes, no TV was allowed at all, even for the sake of the children, and she had met younger couples who would not go to any movie unless it was foreign-made.

Still, none of this quite solved the problem of what to do with the actual time on her hands right now. Ordinarily she would have taken advantage of it to catch up on her ironing, since with Milton having to wear a clean shirt to his classes every day, there were always things piled up from the last wash, even though she had eliminated underwear, pajamas, handkerchiefs, and recently (taking a tip from Julia), her own cotton blouses. (Funny, wasn't it, that in spite of the white house and the trees and the fresh air and all, she should still have to iron shirts, just like Aunt Bessie?) But she had dumped the basket on the dining room table right where Milton was working, and she had promised not to disturb him again. On the other hand, what real harm could it do to tiptoe quietly inside, snatch a few pieces off the top, and be gone before he could ...

"Oh, Jesus!" Milton cried, wheeling around so suddenly he knocked several bluebooks off the table with his elbow. "What are you trying to do, give me heart failure?"

"Take it easy," Tootsie said. "You don't have to make such a production out of it. I was just trying to pick up a few pieces to iron."

"Can't you iron some other time?"

"Okay, I'll iron some other time. Just don't be so nervous."

"*Nervous?*" Milton said. "Listen, who wouldn't be with you climbing all over him? Not to mention the fact that every time I go to mark one of these—" he picked up a few papers and let them drop again "—I find the equations all stuck together with some kind of mashed banana!"

"Now, look here, lover boy," Tootsie said, placing her hands on her hips, "even for you I don't stop feeding the baby. If you want to pay a cleaning lady to iron your shirts for you, that's another story."

"All right, so we'll spend the money on a cleaning lady," Milton said, turning back to his work with a deep sigh. "And this will leave you the free time you need to cultivate your mind."

"Miltie!"

"I'm sorry," Milton said. "I don't know what got into me. I didn't mean it."

"You did mean it. Ever since you got your tenure I'm not good enough for you. I'm never good enough for you."

"Please, Tootsie," Milton said over his shoulder, "don't start that again. I told you I didn't mean it. Let's forget it."

"I would respect you a lot more, Milton Goldfarb, if you weren't such a liar into the bargain."

"What liar?" Milton asked, turning around and spreading his hands helplessly.

"Oh, sure. It was all right when I worked ten lousy years so you could get all your fancy degrees. Then it was, 'Oh, Tootsie, I don't deserve you. Oh, Tootsie, how could I manage without you?' But now that you're a big shot professor, what do you need *me* for?"

"Please, Tootsie," Milton said, getting up and trying to put a soothing hand on her shoulder. "I have to get back to work now. I'm sorry I hurt your feelings before. Honestly. And you know I'll always appreciate what you did for me."

"Yeah, appreciate," Tootsie said, pushing his hand away. "You appreciate George Auerbach's cute little whore that sleeps with him."

"She's not a whore," Milton said. "What do you always want from the kid? Did she ever do you anything?"

"Maybe the next time Dudley comes over with the sporting goods catalogue somebody should remind him what's going on in college houses."

"So now she's bringing in Dudley," Milton explained to a malignant providence. "Tootsie, for the last time I'm warning you—leave Dudley out of this."

"Why? You don't think he laughs himself silly every time he sees you walk out of here with the hunting hat and the long nose and the gun? You don't think in his heart he's saying, 'Oy, look at this kike who thinks I can teach him to be one of us!' No, Milton, it would have been a million times better to keep the chess set and forget about the gun."

"I won't forget about the gun."

"Fine, me too. Bring it in here, and I'll shoot myself in the heart, and we'll be done with it."

"Oh, *shut up!*"

The baby began to cry. The two of them stared at each other transfixed.

"You woke him up," Tootsie said in a hushed voice.

"No, I didn't, Tootsie."

"You made him cry," Tootsie whispered.

"I didn't make him cry."

"You made him cry, you made him cry, you made the baby cry," Tootsie cried helplessly.

"Sh, Tootsie, sh," Milton said anxiously. "It'll be all right. I'll go warm up his bottle. He'll stop in a minute."

"Don't you touch his bottle," Tootsie said sharply. "Don't you lay a finger on it."

"Tootsie, don't be silly. Stop carrying on this way."

The two of them started for the kitchen and colliding in the doorway, reached out and rushed into each other's arms.

"Miltie, Miltie," Tootsie wept. Milton handed her his man's big handkerchief in which she blew her nose with a shuddering sigh.

"I'm sorry," Milton whispered into her hair. "Forgive me, Tootsie. You know I'll always love you." He kissed her on her moist temple as she clung to him. ". . . Miltie, I'm sorry I made you nervous. I won't do it anymore." ". . . it's all right, Tootsie, it's all right. Shsh."

Though the baby screamed louder, Tootsie kept clinging to Milton, comforted by the hardness of him underneath the rough tweed jacket. Little by little her own flesh went slack, and she closed her eyes, trying to feel that Milton had surrounded her. What did the kid ever do to you? Milton had asked. *Plenty, plenty,* her heart cried back. Only she did not say it out loud because she knew it was unreasonable, and Milton hated anything unreasonable.

8

UNFORTUNATELY, the decor of Ye Gorham Inn did not do as much for George as for its other customers, the smooth-faced college boys on their Saturday night dates. Surrounded by antiqued brick and copper warming pans and colonial waitresses rustling back and forth with pewter trays, George sat very stiff and tweedy, with his hair making unruly curls and his necktie climbing towards one ear, so that the gait-legged maple table where they sat was much too small for him. Also he was glaring dreadfully towards the corner where Doris and Leslie and two young men made pale by candlelight had been staring at him since the first course, a quartet of underdone de La Tours, biting when George bit and gulping when he swallowed.

"Winter Carnival Eve at Ye Gorham Inn," George remarked, removing the check from beneath a bowl of Indian pudding.

"How could I know about Winter Carnival Eve?" Daisy said. "It's my first year here."

"Tomorrow, ice skating with the other kids. I wonder sometimes what my future holds in store. Maybe a bring-your-own-bottle party over at the Pilsners'?"

". . . the ice skating was Julia's idea," Daisy said with a slumping of the shoulders, after a moment. "She thought a little fun and fresh air might do you a world of good."

"Oh, great," George said. "I have been smiled on by the Mona Lisa of Gorham. Do thank her for me, won't you?"

"Well, if you prefer the long view," Daisy suggested, "there's always the tradition that poets love nature."

"I didn't realize that questions of métier interested you that much," George said.

"Oh, but they do. In fact you might even say that such a question is at the very core of my being."

"Because in that case," George continued, helping her on with her fur coat, "maybe it's about time you started worrying again about the difference between a long story and a short novel. Oscar Brooks asked me the other day if you have any plans in that direction."

Daisy paused with an arm in one sleeve and glanced at him over her shoulder. Unfortunately he had a point; unfortunately, George was turning out to be one of those people who always had a point. She looked past him towards the leaded Tudor window where a few snow-flakes had begun to hiss and sputter against the dark diamond panes, and glimpsed her own reflection instead of seeing out. Still, she was grateful that aside from wincing and pulling the Indian blanket over his head, George had made no other reference to the unfortunate tea party, although from many points of view she supposed her speech had gone extremely well. At least lots of women had clustered around her afterwards asking if being a good wife and mother wasn't creative too, and what about ceramics? And Stella Brooks had shaken her hand over and over again with a vigorous perspired gratitude that oddly resembled relief. Then, suddenly, it was over. She had walked dully out of President Steel's beautiful mansion, like a child who has been promised a present and received something useful.

Outside on Main Street, beyond the warmth of the huge fireplace, they stood in emptiness for a moment, looking up at a black sky from which flake after flake had begun to criss-cross and swirl in a series of flurries, and then quickly crossed over to the campus and the short cut that George had taught her would take them straight to Elm. In the darkness there was a sweet tinny sound of music, and then through a break in the trees a wet golden circle. Tiny black people skated around and around, so that under the arc lights the scene was beautiful and particular like a little night canvas by Breughel.

"Listen," George said, turning at the touch of her hand on his arm, "instead of plotting with Julia to make an ass of me, why not just write about it?"

"About what?"

"That, for god's sake, the subject that's been staring you right in the face ever since you got here."

"*Where?*"

"I meant," George said, lowering the hand that had been describing a great black sweep against the cobalt blue snow of the mountains, "the contrast between this magnificent, infinite landscape and those puny little people."

"I think they're kind of cute, actually."

"You think everything is kind of cute, actually."

"I've always been partial to miniatures. I also like people. Where's the sin in that?"

"The combination. Listen," George said, "I mean it. The time is fast arriving when you will have to choose between being a novelist and a lollipop."

"But how can I write about something when I don't feel it *here*?" Daisy said. "Any writing course tells you you have to feel it here. And all I feel is intimations of a Breughel. Maybe, some days, a smallish Grandma Moses, but—"

"Daisy, you've been here too long to persist in that lace paper doily view of this town. You can't seriously still think that Stella Brooks is involved in all her projects against her will, or that her prissy-assed husband is at heart a noble gentleman, or that a woman like Julia Lipshansky while basically reserved is still interested in your welfare, because down deep that girl is your natural enemy and don't you forget it, you—"

"But I can't believe you about Julia. In fact, I can't believe you about any of them—except Edgar Dudley, naturally."

"If you were familiar with the work of William Blake," George said, "then you would know—and I quote—that 'Truth cannot be uttered so as to be understood and not be believed,'" and mopped the wet snow off his face as if he had just realized that there was no one to understand much less believe him besides Daisy, who was wearing a curly fur hat that matched her coat and staring at him attentively.

"... George?"

"What?"

"Why do you stay in Gorham if you hate it so much?"

"Who said I hated it?"

"Well, you certainly feel superior to it."

"I am," George said, continuing on. "I'm a first-rate poet in a fifth-rate college for females. But where else do you think I should go?"

"Paris? London? The Fiji Islands?"

"And live on what—coconuts?"

"But don't poets—?"

"Need time to do their work and make a living? Yes, sweetheart, they do. Believe me, if your generation had struggled through the depression the way mine did, you wouldn't take this airy view of my finances."

"We argued about that yesterday, outside of Peck and Peck."

"I know it," George said.

They walked the rest of the way in silence and in silence entered George's apartment and began to undress, like two people in a train compartment, apologizing when they bumped into each other and taking turns in the bathroom. Daisy removed the big pillows from the daybed and folded up the cover. A pair of George's maroon socks were wedged between the blanket and the wall. Sometimes she found them under the seat cushion or behind the books on the shelves. He was always squirreling away his socks, like little dark emotions.

There was a rustle of sheets. "You're not exactly a non-joiner," Daisy remarked to the ceiling. "I even met you at a dinner party—Julia's, in fact."

"Poets have to eat. I can't cook."

"That's true."

"Neither, it turns out, can you."

"That's true too."

86

She gave a short laugh to which, though she turned to him for several moments, George gave no answer.

". . . oh, well," Daisy said, settling herself again, "none of it really matters, does it, when two people love each other? . . . And of course I do love you. . . . I mean, sometimes I love you so much I could die."

"Don't delude yourself," George said, "I'm much too old for you anyway—here," he added, leaning across for a book which he handed to her, "I ordered you an extra copy."

He turned over and in a moment was fast asleep, snoring quietly with one foot in a bright red ski slipper peeping alertly out between the covers. Daisy slowly got out of bed again. No, it was not so easy to give yourself to a man who kept handing you back. And also (she glanced at her present with a sigh—William Atkinson's *Odes to Innocence*—George had autographed this too) . . . well, there were moments when in spite of herself she could not help wondering if George saw her more as his love, or as a kind of comrade-in-arms against foreign ideologies. It was an oddly rigid feeling, like having her feet bound, or finding she had enlisted in the army by mistake, or joined the Roman Catholic Church, an institution, she realized with an even deeper sigh, towards which she had also been drawn at one time. She glanced at George again, who was now making little chugging sounds like an idling train, and for a moment knew exactly where she was, but not how she had got there. A frightening sensation. But it was getting late. She began to gather up her clothes from George's armchair, except for her shoes, which she had to poke for underneath the daybed. Well, how *did* it happen? she asked herself as she headed for the door—and was rewarded with a brief, flickering memory of that eager young girl who had opened her arms wide at Gorham station only to find that Gorham had more or less ducked under them. Did she miss her? No, of course not. The whole joy of life was in outgrowing yourself or other people. And yet, well where was the creature? What had become of her?

She looked behind her, George was sprawled across the entire bed as usual, and closed the door.

The outside hallway was cold. She ran down the creaky stairs quickly, as she did every night, as if they were a bridge between one half of her life and the other. She had left a few lights in her apartment as a welcome to herself, but they were bald and yellow. Her teeth had begun to chatter. She undressed again quickly in the bedroom, fumbling over her body with stiff fingers, and then stuck a few curlers in her hair. But why *couldn't* they sleep in the same bed all night like other couples? (After all, if you looked at it from another angle even nuns wore wedding rings.) Fortunately, as far as George was concerned, it was only a small thought, born of exasperation with the icy country air, and easily dismissed. She climbed between her freezing sheets and turned off the lamp. There was no limit to the darkness. No lights moving softly across the ceiling. No human sound but the bark of a lonely dog. *Oh god*, Daisy thought, *I'm going to die* . . . and reached for the lamp again.

The sudden light caught her like a candid camera, sitting bolt upright in her streaky mirror, clad in the skimpy baby blue nightgown that had been a present from Sylvia, and blinking under the several silver curlers adorning a strangely small head. What was this, tragedy or farce? She started to laugh and began to cry, passing a tender confused hand over her own body. Maybe she was going mad and ought to run out and call for help. But she only made it to the edge of her bed, curling her toes in protest against the cold wooden floor. Oh, Daisy, what's happening to you? Maybe she was *too* happy, yes that was it. Maybe things were going too smoothly, another possibility. After all, she *was* Jewish, though she didn't look it, and Jehovah was a notoriously jealous god, wasn't he? Or maybe it was just all those premature Christmas carols seeping from the dormitories and the toothy Rheingold girls smothering in their own holly. Actually, this was more George's kind of idea than her own, which was perhaps why it comforted her a little. She crawled back between the covers, her heart still palpitating weakly, and decided to go out and buy flannel pajamas tomorrow like George. Good. That would take care of it. She put out the lamp again. But it was one thing to face the fact of dying under a light bulb and another when it was all pitch black. She was only twenty-two years old—*dear god, I'm only twenty-two*—and lost and wandering in a strange country. But was it death itself, she wondered, desperately trying to make an intellectual issue of it, or the idea of oblivion? Would it be so terrible to die if you could only do it knowingly? Suddenly she remembered a television commercial she had once seen over at Tootsie Goldfarb's house. The vivid fatness of the announcer's face. Then the baseball pitcher who came up and blandly threw a ball at him. Then the soldier pumping bullets into his back. Then the automobile screaming towards him. Nothing. He did not move a muscle. He felt nothing, heard nothing, saw nothing. He was protected by an invisible shield that could also protect your teeth. Fade out, long list of credits, the announcer was still fat and smiling. *Oh, no*, Daisy swooned, it can't happen to me. I won't let it. "*Do not go gentle into that good night! Rage, rage against the dying of the light! . . .*" But hadn't he slipped off like a pussycat . . . ?

The next morning, encouraged by the beauty and the hoar frost, she mentioned the matter to George, who shrugged.

"Dylan was a lush."

"Well, yes, but—"

"Although your metaphor about the TV isn't too bad. Maybe you'll be able to use it."

"In what?"

"Never mind," George sighed. "Look, if you think it will bolster up your courage, you can hold onto me the next time it happens. I give you permission."

Impossible, since the problem wouldn't come up unless she were alone, but the solution was so typical of George that she dropped the subject. Also, as a result of the fact that they were now on their way to the rink, he kept glancing at her suspiciously, as if by dying she could involve him forever.

She trudged along behind him, finding his back strangely unfamiliar because of the two heavy sweaters lumping up under his jacket and the noisily flapping galoshes. Why George had decided to go skating after all, she was not sure, only that as often happened, he had stuck his head through her doorway at daybreak and announced the decision as a result of a sleepless night for which she was somehow to blame. At the moment she wished heartily that George had slept better. She had forgotten that today would be Sunday, which was the day his mother had always been most anxious to get him away from his library books into the fresh air with the other children, the day which, especially if the weather were fine, George always spent glued to his desk, typing away feverishly until dusk came and released him from danger. The risk of being out in the open was telling on him acutely. They climbed up one small tangled hillock behind the deserted campus and down another, until George finally leaned against a tree trunk laboring for breath. "Oh, great," George said, "now the stuff is creeping into my galoshes. I can feel my socks freezing to my feet. Which means another week with the vaporizer instead of my work. . . . Not that *you* care."

"Oh, but I do care, I—"

"But why do I always let you talk me into these expeditions?" George said, smiting his forehead. "That's what I don't understand." His skates clanged together against his shoulder and he quickly lowered his arm. "And why above all, do I let myself play December to your May when I know damn well it's an impossible marriage?"

"Marriage?" Daisy said, as the word flew like an arrow into her heart and she plucked it out just as it began to secrete its sweet poisons. "—I mean, you don't have to go, you know."

"No," George smiled grimly, "I don't, do I?" and detached himself from the tree trunk to lead her still muttering down a steep treacherous path, so icy underfoot that they slipped and slid into each other. Straggling branches scratched at their clothing. The path ended abruptly. They started across the frozen churned-up mud of the softball field.

"And don't argue," George said, "until we get the fucking fun over with."

A record of "Jingle Bells" had begun to blare over the loudspeaker, surface scratches and all. Though even without Edgar Dudley's selected background music, the scene at the rink would hardly have inspired George's heart. Everybody in the crowd was either young or a guardian of the young. A few weary faculty wives rocked their lonely perambulators at the edge of the ice while the older children fended for themselves on skates. Otherwise it was all undergraduates, Gorham girls in every shape and size and the boys who had trooped over from Amherst and Williams and Dartmouth to join the fun. More of them were still streaming onto the ice, the girls in flesh-colored tights and short flared skirts, the boys in ski sweaters and knitted caps, the uniforms of the private club they had made of the rink with their hilarity and obliviousness to everyone but each other. Skates slashed, children in snowsuits marched in and out on double runners, a lithe young girl spun figure eights in red velvet. There was a sudden spill, a spray of ice, an ear-splitting squeal. The voices rang out hollowly, like the echoes from the edge of a swimming pool. In the midst of it all, Stella Brooks skated around and around, with her back straight and her eyes fixed on the horizon, and a particularly ruddy and hilarious Edgar Dudley pulled at Milton Goldfarb, who was teetering along on his ankles.

"Well, hello there! Never expected to see you here, George. Glad to have you on board."

Drop dead. Had Edgar Dudley heard him? George did not wait to find out. "Fascinating," he remarked, proceeding to a wet bench and gloomily unslinging his skates, "she confuses Grandma Moses with Hieronymus Bosch, and in addition—" he gave a last bitter twirl to his laces, which immediately snapped off, "beneath her coat she wears a little forest green skating costume. In fact, now that I think of it, a costume for everything. What the hell are you—a paper doll?"

No comment.

George did not expect any. Tucking away his overshoes beneath him tenderly, as if he never expected to see them again, George stood up. As he started towards the ice, he sneezed and a gaggle of girls scattered in his wake like geese.

"Auerbach worshippers," he remarked, almost wistfully. "There was even a faction that refused to believe that I went to the bathroom like other people."

"—George, they can hear you, you know."

"And all these years I've managed to keep a safe and dignified distance from them. But now I am about to plunge myself into their midst. That is, Daisy will plunge—beautifully—while I will make myself ridiculous, which is what I deserve for being talked into this in the first place."

"What do you mean, Daisy will plunge—beautifully?" Daisy said, clomping after him on the splintery wooden walk.

"Well, you look like them, don't you? You dress like them, you act like them, you—"

"That's ridiculous, not to say downright offensive—hello, Doris, how are you this morning?—I've never even laid eyes on these kids before—*oof!*" She had collided with George's back. An earnest young man in a sweater with red reindeer prancing across it, was blinking at George deferentially.

"Excuse me, sir," the young man said with a faint interior clank that made Daisy duck behind George again immediately, "I realize that this is neither the time nor the place to tender my admiration, but I had the pleasure of attending your public reading last week, and I found your comments afterwards on Pound's influence extremely penetrating as well as enjoyable."

"Swell," George said, stepping aside. "Thanks."

"In particular your point that—well, whaddya know! Long time no see! What's new?"

"New?" Daisy said distantly, but not distantly enough.

"The train, the train," the young man said, jogging her memory with a playful poke in the ribs. "You remember." He whipped out his cowbell and cried "Toonerville Trolley!" in a voice that instantly riveted a dozen pair of eyes to them. "So how's the great academic experiment? Pretty snappy—huh, baby?"

"If you'll excuse us—"

"Oh, gosh, sir. I'm sorry. I didn't realize . . ."

There followed several moments of stammering, blushes and confusion while the cowbell was stashed away and an apology tendered to thin air since George had long since whipped Daisy out on the ice and set her on a rigid circular course from which in spite of herself Daisy kept escaping. Somebody had changed the record and they were now all whining around to "White Christmas" at half speed. Good-bye dreams of flying over the ice with her lover as the wind played tricks with their hair. Good-bye flushed cheeks and steaming hot chocolate afterwards.

"There's an awfully nice Rumpelmeyer's on 59th Street," Daisy remarked. "Have you thought at all about going to New York for Christmas?"

"For the pleasure of hearing you say, 'Hello, Mama, this is Georgie'? No, thanks."

"Actually," Daisy said, "as mothers go, she's quite nice. I mean I do come from someplace, you know."

"Really? I thought you were *sui generis*."

It was George's main contention that she never knew when to shut up. She was straining to make a liar out of him. It was not easy. It was even harder to keep in step. Linked young couples kept swooping past to overtake those who were laughing and chattering ahead, and then just in time she avoided little Buddy Lipshansky, who was crawling around underfoot in a fuchsia satin garment made over from god knew what. Wobble, wobble, glide, glide—"oh, sorry"—only George's iron grip kept the two of them from sliding apart permanently, like an example of Newton's law of eternal momentum.

"Of course," George remarked, yanking her back for the fifth or sixth time, "the fascinating thing to me is that your friend, by which I mean Whizzbang the Cowbell, appears to speak two varieties of English simultaneously."

"He's not my friend. I just met him on a train once."

"Oh? I thought that perhaps there was an implied intimacy."

"With *him*?"

"After all, how would I know?"

"Now, look here, George—"

"My, my," George said. "Don't we sound like our sister."

"You never met my sister either."

"I don't have to. I see her in my mind's eye with hideous clarity. Her husband wears a pocket handkerchief that matches his socks."

"George, everybody's watching us, as usual."

"Good, they need a catharsis anyway. Pity and terror. It will loosen their bowels."

"Oh, why can't you be a little more human, like other people?" Daisy cried.

"What other people?"

"Oh, I don't know. Seymour Lipshansky, I guess, or—"

"*Seymour?*" George repeated in a strangled voice. "Did I understand you to say that you now wish me to model myself after *Seymour?*"

"No, of course not. I only meant—"

But no. It was clear that short of hitting George over the head with a frying pan, she could not have stunned or horrified him more. Oblivious to everyone who was trying to skate by them, he had stopped dead in his tracks to give her a look that came straight from the depths of his startling gray-green eyes and chilled her to the marrow. Daisy stared back at him helplessly, perfectly aware that in that crowd they must have resembled two figures caught in a Greek frieze, and that if fate did not intervene they would probably stand there forever, stony and immutable, one of the tourist attractions of Gorham. But fate did intervene, choosing hideously the person of little Buddy Lipshansky who crawled between their skates with joyous abandon. He tugged at George's trouser leg.

It occurred to Daisy fleetingly that a lesser man might have gone down right then and there. Not George Auerbach. Like a slow-motion movie played in reverse, he proceeded to stagger backwards. A moment later, he was still going, cutting a wide swath between the skaters, including Stella Brooks, who parted with unconcealed fascination to let him pass. It was Whizzbang, of course, who provided the ultimate obstacle, and down whose legs George slid with a last sickening thump. But was it Whizzbang who laughed first, working his Adam's apple so frantically that what emerged was a short sharp bark? Or Julia Lipshansky abandoning her silent smile for once and pealing with laughter as she scooped up her little Buddy? Whoever it was, it went around the group like wildfire.

George was very nice about it. He sat drumming his fingers on the ice until everyone was finished and then stood up and brushed the wet off his pants. "Au revoir, Miss Lerner," he said, tipping his hat pleasantly.

"Wait a minute, George, I'll come with you."

"Don't bother. No fun and games. I'm only going home to bed—with my cold."

"I'll bring you some soup."

"You'll bring me nothing."

"George, I do wish you wouldn't take this attitude."

"*You* speak to *me* of *attitudes*?" George said. "When all these hyenas were laughing, who was laughing the loudest?"

"Me. But it was just a reflex action. I mean I can't help it. Whenever I see something terribly funny, I—oho! ha ha! . . . "

"To quote the poet Dante," George said bitterly, "*la commedia e finita.*"

"But, darling, surely you—"

She had raised her hand in a gesture of entreaty, but now closely scrutinized by a group of intent undergraduates and a highly amused Julia Lipshansky, she quickly converted it into a casual flip of farewell.

9

IT WAS DIFFICULT, no impossible, to believe that the same man who had slid clear across the skating rink this morning was also the spirit behind the dignified display in the bookstore window. Yet there was the evidence, twenty or so slim white volumes pyramided on each other, with simple black lettering in which George's name was suitably subordinated to the whole: *The Complete Poems of Amelia Lacey*, ed. and with an intro. by George Auerbach. A perfect example, Stella Brooks thought, almost forgetting she had arranged for it in the first place, that one had to take the rough along with the smooth. (A point she must make to poor Sue Carp, by the way, who now needed to be endlessly reassured that writing cookbooks *was* creative. As if that were the main issue, when as she had told Oscar afterwards, it had all been such a *parody* of everything they held dear.) But it was wrong to brood on this dazzling day when even the snow, no doubt ground to thick gray mush in other places, was still in its pristine state in Gorham, and the sidewalk reflected the sunshine with a thousand brilliant pinpoints. For a few moments, Stella Brooks let herself bask in her achievement, as the girls swept on past her, wafting bits of conversation into the crisp clear air—". . . but I mean, why would a man like that allow that kind of thing to happen in the first place?" ". . . well, I think it's more a question of when she's only thirty doesn't she realize he'll be practically *fifty*?"—and finally tore herself away to drive home and continue with all the other necessary arrangements for the Memorial Ceremony, such as seeing to it that the executors of the Lacey estate gave permission to open the gates of the family plot again this year, and that the president of the Rotary Club held his speech down to fifteen minutes.

No, there was no doubt that the tribute to Amelia meant more work and heavier responsibilities than all Stella's other projects put together. And yet, in twenty busy happy years in Gorham, she had also found it the most richly rewarding, the only event sponsored by the college in which the natives took part willingly, probably out of the feeling that with Amelia Lacey a local girl and Stella Brooks a faculty wife, it was a kind of tribute from gown to town. Not that it was as simple as it sounded. Certainly not, Stella Brooks thought, stripping a gear so energetically that out on the white country road a rabbit popped out of its hedge to inquire. Even on an occasion as noble as this, one met the usual malcontents and the usual carping criticisms, mainly from a few of the younger wives whose children had caught cold the year before and who could not understand why Stella Brooks refused to move the Annual Songfest, which was celebrated in a heated auditorium, over to the wintertime, and reschedule the Ceremony, which now had them congregated around the poetess's frozen grave, for the late spring. But fortunately they were an unimportant group and no one paid them much attention, least of all Stella Brooks. "But how little it is to ask of ourselves," she had said, turning towards two such young women the last time they approached her directly (which was very rare) with a smile of gentle disappointment, "when you consider how she gave her all to us. That we in the decades to come—" And then, feeling that she had gone too far and possibly wasted what might do very well in her address, had ended with a little wave of the hand, as if she were leaving the rest to the judgment of posterity. Privately, of course, she had no doubt as to whether she or the faint hearts would be vindicated. No, it was easy enough to remember Amelia in the spring and in the long summer days, and everyone did—tourists, busloads of school children, beer-drinking picnickers (she shuddered to think who else)—but who but Stella Brooks remembered, when the snow was thick and an icy wind blew through leafless trees, that poor Amelia slept alone in her cold, cold grave? It was enough to make a person weep, and she often did. "Oh, for Christ's sake, cheer up, Stella," George Auerbach had once told her with a sickening thump on the back, "would you be any happier if she slept *with* someone?" but after the look she gave him, even he, she was proud to say, had never tried it again.

Parking the station wagon, Mrs. Brooks sailed on through the redwood carport, and allowed herself time out for a word or two with Mrs. Baines, who was complaining again that it made her dizzy to work in a house on stilts and also how could a person clean the woodwork when there was no woodwork? "Yes, of course I appreciate your point," she laughed. "At heart I'm just an old-fashioned girl too. But like it or not we do have to keep up with the times, now don't we?" To which Mrs. Baines agreed so readily that Stella Brooks quickly looked to see if Oscar had heard, before she turned her mind to the next problem: what she should wear to the actual ceremony itself that would be both warm and appropriate. Not a serious question, naturally, and of course even Amelia Lacey must have faced similar ones in her own life, unless she wore those white dresses day in and day out, which was very hard to believe. But enough to send her downstairs to rummage through the old trunk in the combination storage basement and playroom (the modern architect had point-blank refused them an attic).

Shabby and half-hidden by the new ping-pong table and the knotty-pine wall paneling, the little trunk seemed to reproach her for having put it there in the first place. She walked over to it gingerly, and raised the lid to a troubled squeak of hinges. But a treasure awaited right on top. She shook it out, coughing from the sudden swarm of dust motes in the air, and uncertain how she would describe it to Sue Carp. A capelet perhaps? No, a trifle short. A tippet then? Alas, too long. Which was a terrible shame, really, since the word tripped so poetically off the tongue, it would have been a pleasure to wear one. In any case, it was in excellent shape, black velour, with a standing collar of orange fox. She put it on, and hurried upstairs to find a mirror, pausing impulsively at the pointed archway of her husband's study.

"Oscar, for the Ceremony. I know that people may think it a bit *de trop*, but—?"

If the look on Edgar Dudley's face was any indication, the answer was *yes!* though why he was there and why his eyes appeared to be rooted to her person in a kind of paralyzed fascination, she had no idea.

"Oh, well," Stella Brooks said, trying to smile graciously, "I don't need to decide right away."

"Nonsense, my dear," Professor Brooks said, with a short glance at Dudley. "It's charming. Very much in keeping with the occasion. . . . Of course, you might want to, perhaps, trim the fur border a little?"

"Yeah," Edgar Dudley said, coming to with a start.

"Do you think so?" Mrs. Brooks said, groping eagerly around her ears for stray wisps. "Better than to give it up altogether? I mean—" She had knocked the collar down accidentally, leaving herself feeling very drafty about the head and curiously defenseless. "You're sure you're not just being kind, both of you?" she said dubiously. "—actually, all I had in mind was—"

"A tribute to a major poet," Professor Brooks smiled. "A small but altogether major poet."

"Not like old Georgie, huh?" Edgar Dudley laughed.

"George?" Stella Brooks repeated in a voice gone suddenly dull. "Are we talking about George *again*?"

"I'm afraid so," Professor Brooks said.

In the moment of silence that followed Edgar Dudley sighed and lowered his head, after which he leaned forward again enthusiastically. "Listen," he said with a wheedling smile, "I know you folks aren't interested in the housing situation. I know you have your minds on higher things—" "As indeed we do," Stella Brooks agreed so readily that he took advantage of the moment to ask how the new stove was coming along and waiting to make sure neither of them was going to answer him.

"—but on the other hand," he continued, "just to get back to the main point for a minute, Oscar. Number one, let me remind you it was your department that invited this Englishman in the first place. . . . Number two, the girl has the only expendable apartment for the six weeks the guy is going to be around. . . . Number three, you're the only people with a spare room for *her*. . . . Number four—"

"Look here, Edgar," Professor Brooks interrupted, clearing his throat, "are you certain you've explored all the other possibilities—for Mr. Atkinson, I mean? Does he really need an entire apartment, for example? Wouldn't the Inn do just as well?"

"On the dough you people are paying him?" Edgar Dudley said. "Oscar, let's level with each other. I've been burning the midnight oil on this thing, and speaking frankly—"

"Because of course, George is at the bottom of it all," Professor Brooks said with an ironic twist of the lips.

"Sure he is," Edgar Dudley laughed. "Who the hell doesn't know that by now? By god, if I could sell either one of them a car, I swear to you they could never be so open about it."

"I meant," Professor Brooks murmured, focusing his eyes on a painful point in the middle distance, "the invitation to Mr. Atkinson to give the seminars in the first place."

"Oh—and you really think that for six weeks even for the sake of literature, George wouldn't be willing to—?" Edgar Dudley looked around, as if he had suddenly become conscious that the point included himself. "Yeah, I see what you mean. No cold showers for this boy. . . ." He slapped his leg thoughtfully. "Well, no need to make any snap decisions."

"No."

"On the other hand, Oscar," Edgar Dudley added, giving him a jovial sock in the arm, "from what I saw down at the rink today, it's possible George is just about ready to unload that Tootsie Roll. Maybe he'll even be grateful to you. Who knows? Remember what we're dealing with here is a race of overachievers."

Professor Brooks assured him he would remember, and after he had seen him out the door, returned some moments later to sit down heavily in his chair and rub his arm.

". . . No," Professor Brooks said at last, "no, as things stand there's absolutely no question George would be adamant against—"

"Adamant?" Stella Brooks repeated, who as Edgar Dudley had suggested had been trying to comfort herself with higher thoughts as she blew into her fox. "Ought we all to forget that this is a college for young ladies?"

"On the contrary. It's a point I think we can trust Edgar to come down on heavily, almost with a smacking of the lips, one might say."

"Yes, but still, Oscar—"

"Whereas, *I*, my dear," he corrected her gently, "was rather more concerned with *our* sensibilities, even if it is for a comparatively short time."

Accepting the correction with a troubled nod and a deep sigh, Stella Brooks sat down on the arm of her husband's chair and for a very long while gazed through the picture window at their silent, snow-covered garden and the neat green stand of fir trees just beyond it.

"Oh, look, Oscar, a deer!"

In the brilliant sunshine the tiny animal was stark and fragile against the snow. He stood as still as a picture, listening for an invisible click, and then blinked and bounded nearer the house, ducking his head and nibbling about the snowy stumps of last year's rhododendrons. Except that Professor Brooks was frowning uneasily and paying no attention.

"On the other hand," he said, wiping his pate with an immaculate handkerchief, "I suppose it is about time I called George into my office and discussed the entire matter with him. . . . Put it to him strongly. . . . Yes, very strongly."

"Well, perhaps not *too* strongly, dearest," Mrs. Brooks said with a cautionary smile, as she busied herself with the capelet again and tried for a more artful arrangement of its folds. "Perhaps the best thing would be merely to ask him in for some sherry after the Ceremony with William, and maybe the Carps too, and possibly Henrietta Badger—yes, that would make a very good group, wouldn't it? And then you could simply draw him aside for a moment and point out—very discreetly, of course—how those nice young men from the art department always manage these things."

She looked up. The deer had moved so close that except for the wall of glass they could have put out a hand to touch him, and now he moseyed even nearer, looking at them with velvet loving eyes.

"Oh, see how *tame* he is!" Stella Brooks cried. "See how he *trusts* us!"

"Okay," Tootsie said, turning to Milton when the fifth they might have nursed along for months had been drained, and snow stamped all over the welcome mat, also to Tootsie's horror, though she should have been used to it by now. "So maybe the original suggestion shouldn't have come from me. Maybe it wasn't exactly my business. But did I commit such a crime?"

"Look," Milton said. "You have your opinions, I have mine. Let's call it a democracy and let it go at that, all right?"

"Some democracy," Tootsie said. "Some opinions."

"So go tell your friend on me too."

"My friend?" Tootsie said, stabbing herself in the breast with astonishment. "Since when is he my friend?"

"Excuse me. I thought maybe the way he was hanging around, that's what he was."

"Am I the one who goes hunting with that horse's ass? Am I the one who traded in the chess set?"

"The hunting season," Milton assured her, "is over."

"And I suppose the housing season is over too? And I suppose if I ever get a bigger place out of him with a nice study for you, you won't move into it? Who was I doing it for anyway? Myself?"

"Tootsie," Milton said sadly, "you won't believe this, but I'm beginning to think maybe I'd be better off without your favors," and gathering up his papers, went off to the dining room, closing the door firmly behind him.

Sanctuary, as both of them knew perfectly well. It was just an ordinary door with a slapdash coat of brown varnish, courtesy of Edgar Dudley, but it might just as well have been cast in bronze and ornamented with gargoyles for all the good it did her. No, Tootsie thought, staring at it with hot, tear-filled eyes, she had never gone in there on purpose to aggravate Milton when he was working and she could not do it now, even though God knew she had ample reason, even though a lump of ice was forming in her chest big enough to choke a horse. "Come here, doll," she murmured, wrenching the baby out of the teeter babe where he had fallen asleep with his head in the tray during Dudley's visit, poor thing, and holding him tight against her for a little comfort. But although his breath was warm and moist on her cheek and she was even wearing the bulky tan fruitman's sweater that Julia Lipshansky had encouraged her to buy at the local rummage sale, she was still trembling. Outside in the back the Negro children were whooping it up again. They were the only ones in town and they had to come and play in her yard, of all places, so that she could not even complain to Dudley out of the fear that he would take them as some kind of black mark on her housing record. But she did not even bother to go and chase them. Was it possible, was it really possible? Her whole youth people had always remarked on how good Tootsie was, "*too* good," they always said. And now, she thought with a bitter stab of pain, even Milton Goldfarb was telling her he could live without her favors.

10

THE SPINY TREES THAT MET OVERHEAD in the bleak winter
sunshine looked down at Daisy reproachfully, much the way George
would look when she finally got home, since in addition to raging over
his pratfall he was undoubtedly nursing a cold by now. Also, although
the air was unseasonably mild, for once in her life Daisy realized
that it was only an indication of more snow instead of, as she used
to tell herself, a poignant reminder of spring. She wrapped her fur
coat tightly around her and buried her chin in its silky collar, trying
to ignore the drip of melted ice down her neck from the skates slung
around it and the fact that after George had been placated she would
probably be up until midnight marking freshman compositions for
tomorrow. How strange. She had never really been troubled by the
future before, only the immediate present, and at the end of a movie
always swooned and faded away with the lovers, not to have it dawn
on her for months afterwards that they had surely set up housekeep-
ing by now and were fighting like cats and dogs. But now, she had an
increasingly dark suspicion that the future was about to catch up with
her. Still, *Amor Omnia Vincit*. Even the brooch on the prioress's breast
had proclaimed it. . . . But suppose it didn't? No, it was only the letter

from Sylvia accompanying the baby doll pajamas which had shaken her confidence a little (but, why *did* Sylvia's name keep popping up so often lately?), that and the repeated references to *Marjorie Morningstar*, which she could no longer ignore. ". . . so that Lou and Mama and I are confident that whatever this phase is, you'll get over it and settle down and have adorable children. . . ." No, George was right, as usual, though for the wrong reasons. A trip to New York would be no solution at all (a couple of days trying on the new mutation silver-blu minks, a few encounters in the hall with the brother-in-law), the coward's way out, in fact.

As a passing car slowed down to give her a lift—nothing seemed to upset and startle the natives of Gorham quite so much as a pedestrian—Daisy waved it on, wishing she had the nerve to drop in on people unannounced the way everyone else did. Even the Lipshansky house a few yards further down looked strangely inviting, flaking gray dilapidated ruin that it was, and Julia herself had urged her before she drove laughing from the rink to drop by and cheer Seymour up, a very ambiguous invitation, come to think of it. Before she could actually give it much thought, there was a sudden heavy screech of snow tires and a splash of clotted ice against her legs. The car, a flashy and repellent green Thunderbird, had made a U-turn and stopped for her anyway.

"Well, well, well," Edgar Dudley boomed, sticking his head out of the window. "Speak of the devil—"

"Oh?" Daisy said in a dying voice. "You were talking about me?"

"Figure of speech," he explained shortly. "You literary types are supposed to know all about that. Whoa, there, little lady. How about a lift?"

"That's very kind of you, Mr. Dudley, but I—"

"Mr. Dudley's my father. I'm Eddie."

Eddie Dudley? It reminded her of an old joke about a man who told his butcher, "I said kidleys, diddle I?" But she was not laughing as much, or as easily, as she used to.

"That's right," he said, opening his door. "No need to be snooty. We're all friends here."

"Oh, but I—"

Was it Tootsie Goldfarb who always said that Edgar Dudley was no man to argue with? How it happened, she was not sure, but within a moment she was sitting on the cold leather seat right beside him, staring at the glittering dashboard like his copilot. "Okay, little lady," Edgar Dudley said, pulling on a pair of brand new pigskin gloves and smelling strongly of bourbon as he revved up the motor. "We'll have you home in no time."

"Home?" Daisy said. "Yes, well, actually, I'm not really in such a hurry to get there. In fact, I was just sort of slowly walking along when you—"

"Slowly walking? In the middle of winter? Honest to Christ, it's a wonder some of you city people know enough to come in out of the rain."

He shook his head at her for a moment until his incredulity finally overcame disgust. "Okay, okay, I'll tell you what. Suppose we just take us a nice little spin around the block and have us a nice little talk. No point in bringing you in out of the cold if I can't warm you up a little bit, is there?" He laughed. "And if anybody finds us, like Mrs. Dudley, for instance—" Huge wink.

Daisy moved closer to the window in spite of the dry frost it exhaled on her cheek. Over to the west, thick black smoke poured from a factory chimney into an otherwise light blue sky. It came from a part of town no one ever seemed to mention, where she had gone a few times to have beer with George, a neighborhood of saloons and neon signs and pizza parlors, where the children played in the refuse and tumbleweeds of vacant lots.

"Yup, that factory supports a lot of them," Edgar Dudley said, cocking his head slightly. "The old cemetery's down that way too, a mile or so further on. You'll see it at the Amelia Lacey thing."

"I will?"

"Oh, sure. There's still lots of things about this town you haven't seen or even heard of yet that you'll want to look into, am I right? Like all those very fine antique shops out on Route 6, near the Tastee Freeze stand. That's the kind of thing you'll want to bear in mind when you fix up a house of your own."

"Am I fixing up a house of my own?"

"Well, you don't want to depend on college housing all your life, do you?"

"No, I suppose not, but—"

"Hell, no," he chuckled. "As soon as the two of you set the date, you come to me and we'll start looking for a nice little piece of property. I'll get you a damn good buy too. Why keep renting from the college? As soon as your husband retires or dies—out you go. All that money wasted and nothing to show for it. No sir, the answer for you, little lady—"

"But I'm not getting *married*," Daisy said.

"Oh?" Edgar Dudley said, swerving around the corner and cutting his motor dead. "Are you sure about that, or are you just trying to con me, or what?"

"Con you?" Daisy said. "On the contrary. Oops, I'm sorry, that one just slipped out . . . I mean—"

She tried to smile, but his red pensive face was fixed on her.

"We're only friends . . ." Daisy murmured, speaking with some difficulty through frozen cheeks.

It was a piece of news that caused Edgar Dudley to break into a sudden and amazing crash of laughter.

"Not brawny enough, eh?" he guffawed, subsiding a little and wiping tears of sympathy from the corners of his eyes. "Christ, I don't blame you. That was quite a sight down at the rink." He sobered up for a moment. "But I didn't think that would bother you as long as he had it up here. Upstairs—that's what you people cared most about, I heard."

"Which people?"

"*Which* people?" Edgar Dudley said, throwing his head back and roaring again. "And looking at me with those big baby-blue eyes! . . . That's okay. . . . Yessir, I told you the first time I saw you I like a girl with a good sense of humor. We'll get along just fine. Yes indeedy, everything's going to work out fine and dandy."

He stopped fiddling with the ignition and moved closer, spraying Daisy with a confidential mixture of spit and whisky. "Meanwhile, if anything bothers you, if you get discontented or lonesome, you just come to old Uncle Eddie and we'll see what we can do."

"Good-bye, Mr. Dudley," Daisy said, removing his hand from her knee.

His smile froze. "Hey, now wait a minute, Miss. It's about time you got with it. This happens to be a great little town and it's got some great little people living in it. But just because they're nice and friendly doesn't mean they're a bunch of yokels and you can go around pulling the wool over their eyes."

Daisy reached for the door handle.

"There are rules every place," Edgar Dudley said. "Maybe not where *you* come from, but just about everywhere else. Now, maybe you don't like those rules. That's your business. But if you want to get along here, you'll just have to put up with them like everybody else. Now, don't get me wrong. Nobody gives a damn what you do or who in hell you do it with. But once people start talking—and believe me, little lady, you've got them talking—it's up to *me* whether you do it in college property."

The car door, which after a struggle Daisy had finally succeeded in opening, slammed shut in Dudley's face. "Hey, what are you getting sore about?" he called, hastily rolling down the window. "Nothing's so serious it can't be worked out between friends."

She ran breathlessly and apologetically up the Lipshansky steps, assuming at first that the house was empty because of the punching bag dangling motionless and disconsolate in the living room archway. And then, as she stayed a moment, stilling her heart with her hand, her eyes accustomed themselves to the dimness and she saw a huddled shape at the end of the sofa and Seymour's feet sticking up on the coffee table, bare and bony like the trees in the frozen New England countryside behind him.

"Oh, hi," Seymour said, glancing up and pulling together the edges of his bathrobe. "I hear big boy took a real flop on his ass today. Come on in and tell me your version."

"If you don't mind, Seymour," Daisy said, ignoring the place he was patting beside him on the sofa and choosing a saggy armchair near the fireplace, "I think I'd like to be the one person in town who doesn't discuss it." There was a book open on the floor. *Seven Types of Ambiguity*. Seymour seemed to have given up on the *Third*. She stuck her hands in her pockets and curled up like a chilly cat. ". . . where's Julia, by the way?"

"Over at the Pilsners' with the kids. Or was she taking them to Dr. Rust's first? I'm not sure."

"Oh? Buddy wasn't hurt or anything, was he?"

"No, no, nothing like that. They've got bronchitis or something, that's all. They're always sick all winter."

"Yes, that's right," Daisy nodded. "I keep forgetting." She blanketed her coat more tightly around her. "You know something, Seymour? It's awful to say this, but I'm beginning to hate this town, I think."

"You sound like George."

"No, this time it's my own idea. You'll be glad to hear that I just slammed a door in Edgar Dudley's face."

"Oh, Jesus," Seymour said, sounding very worried. "What did you want to go and do a thing like that for?"

"Well, he had his hand on my leg, for one thing."

"Couldn't you have been nicer about it?"

"*Nicer?* Seymour, please can the comedy. I'm still shaking from the encounter. Anyhow, I thought you detested him."

"That's not the point. Now you've only antagonized the bastard."

"I hope so. He certainly antagonized me."

"Listen," Seymour sighed impatiently, "life is tough enough as it is. You don't have to invite trouble. Next time you see him, you'd better try to butter him up, laugh the whole thing off."

"Seymour, you may not realize it, but that happens to be pretty disgusting advice."

"Oh?" Seymour said. "I didn't know you thought I was so disgusting."

"Seymour, never mind the red herrings for a minute. The man insulted me. You advise caution. I'm concerned with self-respect."

"And you don't think I have any?"

"Listen," Daisy said, "which one of us are we talking about, anyway?"

Seymour gloomily asked her for a cigarette and she gloomily tossed him the rest of her pack, hurrying to put her hands back into her pockets. It was always colder in Seymour's house than anywhere else, and though by now she knew all about the high price of oil, she could not help feeling sorry for all the poor sick children who lived here, and by a sort of illogical extension—she was shivering—for herself too. She had expected Seymour to be more sympathetic, or at least maybe to light the fire.

"No, really. Why *is* everyone so concerned with everyone else? And why do they always act as if living in Gorham were a reward instead of a process?"

"Bullshit."

"But it's true. There are cold eyes everywhere. Some days it's pure 1984, almost. I see Edgar Dudley and he tells me he's afraid of what people are saying about me. I see you and you're worried about how I act towards Edgar Dudley. You see? It's sinister."

"You're confused," Seymour advised her. "Also very unrealistic."

"When I was young," Daisy said, "people used to tell me I'd understand when I grew up. Now that I still don't understand, I'm unrealistic. What's unrealistic about wanting people to be joyful and free? What's unrealistic about wanting people to open their hearts to the truth instead of each other's opinions?"

"It's not a question of opening hearts, for Christ's sake. You go around saying anything that's on your mind you can hurt a lot of people. Anyhow, how do you know the truth?"

"Seymour, truth and beauty are deep within every human being if only they probe deeply enough."

"George Auerbach, *op. cit.*"

"I do wish you wouldn't keep saying that," Daisy said. "It's not very flattering, you know." She glanced at him thoughtfully. "Do you really think it sounds like George? Oh, hell, Seymour, what are we arguing about, anyway? I just wish people around here were a little freer, braver, gutsier, that's all. Look, I have to go home."

"Well," Seymour said, giving her a smile mixed with pity and fatigue and also an infuriating touch of condescension, "let's hope you still have all your fine ideals in about ten years, when you have a houseful of kids and no dough and a husband who needs his job."

"I'll say the same things and I'll take the same risks."

"Life hasn't trapped you yet," Seymour smiled, "but it will."

"My god, I'd sooner *die* than blame life for my own kids and my own laziness and my own failure and my own—"

She stopped short, blinking suddenly as if the bright lights of a play had been cut off, leaving her in the foolish gray day of reality. Seymour was all hunched up against the icy window, looking as if she had pricked a hole in his side and let the air out of him.

"Oh, Seymour, I—"

"You get it from George," Seymour said in a low voice. "He despises everyone."

"Why keep bringing George into it? He—"

"You used to be so sweet before with that fluffy blond hair. Now I hardly ever see you anymore."

"I still have blond hair."

"I know it," Seymour said, more depressed than ever.

"Now, look, Seymour, you're the keeper of lost souls around here. If you think I've gone astray, why don't you tell me how?"

"Go ask George."

"All right," Daisy said, "I will," and rose with some dignity, only to find herself slumped back in the chair a moment afterwards, like Seymour's twin sister. Except that she could never endure this house day after day and the bone-dry splintery life Seymour eked out in it. What must it feel like always to have those pale owl eyes pressed against the glass while everyone else was eating? It was a terrible price to pay for eternal youth. She heard the porch steps creak and groan, and thought that Julia must have returned with the children, but then the tortured sounds subsided and she realized that the whole day had drained away. It was all nearly extinguished, the broken toys, the angular furniture, and even herself in this corner—they were tipped on the mournful brink of evening. *Forlorn, forlorn, the very word tolled like a bell.* George again? No, Keats, thank god.

"Seymour?" she said softly.

"What?"

"I just wanted to say I'm sorry."

"What are you sorry about?"

"Everything. I made a mean crack before. I apologize."

"Forget it."

"No."

"Anyhow," Seymour murmured to the windowpane, "you're right. Why kid myself? I know I'm just a lousy flop and a coward."

"I didn't say that."

"Why not? It's true. Don't you think it eats at me all the time, like a cancer?"

"Please, Seymour, I beg you not to talk like that. I said I was sorry."

"Okay, forget it," Seymour whispered wretchedly, turning an all but invisible face towards her except for the faintly glinting eyeglasses.

A curious sickness brooded between them. Why, the poor darling, Daisy thought, staring at him thunderstruck. And then: how could I have forsaken him so long?

11

THE FIRST THING TO AWAKEN GEORGE from his troubled sleep
was the thumping of the radiator in the corner because for a moment
he had mistaken it for footsteps. And then the vaporizer, which he
had bought and kept lovingly by his side ever since his first winter in
Gorham eight years before, though it had never been a particularly
efficient machine, began to tap the electricity so that the gooseneck
lamp on George's work table flickered painfully, even through his
tightly closed eyelids. He opened them reluctantly, unwilling to get
up from this couch (which he now thought of familiarly as his bed of
pain) and where he had flung himself down as soon as he had come
home that morning and remained fully clothed ever since. Except that
a few times he had arisen to make a little halfhearted mess here and
there so that his Indian blanket and the floor around him were strewn
with such items as the torn envelopes from yesterday's mail (including
the bill from his son's school forwarded with the usual offensive note
from his wife, now a volunteer social worker; a couple of invitations
for readings from other schools in the Green Valley area; and a suggestion from some idiot editor that he do an article on William Atkinson or that William Atkinson do an article on him, he had already

forgotten which) . . . Also, now that he was leaning on an elbow, and looking around more closely, a dirty pair of galoshes, a hockey skate with broken yellow laces, and—George let himself sink back again—a copy of the *Selected Poems* which had landed backside up to show the appreciative blurb George had written about himself and the astonished photograph taken early in his career when he apparently used to suck an empty pipe against a backdrop of books.

For a little while longer, George allowed himself to remain in that cloudy tasteless sleep peculiar to a cold, though he was also grimly aware of the smell of burned soup from his kitchen, and the fact that the pot in which it had dried to a black sediment now crowned a whole pile of dirty dishes in the sink. And then, as the flickering of the gooseneck lamp grew worse, and the silver radiator in the corner contracted and thumped more violently against the loss of its heat, he sat up—what time was it anyway, four? Five?—scratching his chin where the coarse Indian blanket had made it itch, and pulling down his jacket and shirt, which had bunched up on him. From this position, his room seemed an even worse shambles than before, and also, on account of the bourbon he had been dosing himself with, somewhat cloudy and cockeyed. He let his smarting eyes rest for a moment on the overturned ice skate. Damn her, he wondered, taking a quick swig from the bottle at his side, what was keeping her anyway? And realized the minute he had swallowed, that alcohol in his present state was a mixed blessing since while its fumes cleared his head, they also left him wide open to a new assault from the burned soup that stank in the kitchen. He sneezed a few times, tossing the Kleenex into an already overflowing brown paper bag, and laughed to himself bitterly. *Soup? Footsteps?* Even an idiot would have realized by now that she was taking him at his word and leaving him strictly alone. And actually the more he thought about it, the happier he was that it had all turned out this way. Yes, it was better, far better (and nobler too) to die of loneliness and neglect than be murdered by the hand of a child fanatic. In fact, he no longer even blamed her as, well to be honest about it, he had for a chilly moment or two there on his return from the rink. Because after all, what could such a healthy self-centered young animal understand of sickness and despair? Why, it had probably not even flickered through her sugar-frosted mind for a moment that after the events of such a day her aging lover might be lying desolate with a head full of gas and possible catarrh of the lungs. No, what really pained and puzzled him was not so much Daisy's heedlessness of his feelings—god knew there had been sufficient evidence of that before—but how he, George Auerbach, poet, dreamer, lyric singer, sonneteer, could have become so tangled up with such an incredibly literal-minded girl. "No soup? All right, dear, no soup," George squeaked aloud in a sore-throated falsetto. And she, no doubt, was busy downstairs thinking how adorable she was!

For a brief moment he had a vision of himself sitting in sodden trousers on a bed of ice while above a pair of innocent blue eyes and outstretched mittened hands entreated him, and closed his mind against it as quickly as it had come. No, because weren't they all beautiful and beckoning in the beginning, even his almost ex-wife, now so happily victimizing the poor. ("Gary is doing very well at school. His teachers tell me he has a very outgoing personality, which is very unusual in a child of separated parents, as I know from my own work with such offspring." Which was more nauseating, her use of the word "offspring" or that she should call it work? Oh, the incredible *chuzpah* of the woman!) Even the chittering locusts out there—wasn't that the whole trick of it, in fact? And then when they had stuck those little round pink tits in a man's face and heard him cry "Mama!" that was when they all buttoned up again in horror. A tired smile crossed George's face as he gathered up the tattered rags of his pride. Could this mean that at last George Auerbach understood Freud as well as Freud understood him? No, probably not, he thought, taking another drink and lying down again, and also the effort had exhausted him.

He pulled the Indian blanket over his head, rejoicing in its scratchy blackness. Work and solitude, solitude and work. This was what it always came down to in the end. Except—he groaned aloud—even a dedicated hermit like Thoreau would have held up his hands against the isolation of a cold like the one this was turning out to be. This awful, blunted blurring of the mind, this soundless scentless sickness of the senses. Not even another human being to reach out and touch. The black end of the rainbow. Well, maybe there was a poem in it. He got up wearily and went over to his typewriter, where he screwed a yellow sheet into the roller. *Pariah!* George thought, wiping his nose on his sleeve and resting a fevered head on the keys. They would wait for it weeping in anticipation, as they had waited on the docks for news of Little Nell.

It was the dogs barking raggedly beneath his window that roused him next, a few moments later. That there were two of them, large and brown and shaggy, trying to scale the walls of the house though they had been tied to the porch railing, George knew without stirring from the couch where he had laid himself down once more, just as he knew in intimate detail the identity of their owner. In fact, he had been expecting this visit every day for so long, he had almost forgotten it was really possible, though of course it was exactly like that bland bitch to have chosen a time when she knew he would be feeling like hell, taking a certain private satisfaction, he imagined, in making him play tragedy with a running nose. As if Oedipus had sneezed before he did the bloody deed, as if the fleeing Orestes had borrowed a handkerchief from one of the furies. When Julia entered, George barely bothered to turn his head.

"Look, if you want to do something constructive," he sighed dismally, "why don't you clean this place up? There's a whole pile of dishes in the sink."

"All right, would you really like me to do them?"

"No. Why did you have to bring the dogs?"

"I'm out walking them," Julia laughed. "What else would I be doing alone on such a cold evening while my children are playing at the Pilsners'?"

"Trying to notify the whole neighborhood of this little visit, I suppose. It's the classic revenge, isn't it? Bringing the house down on everyone's head?"

"My goodness, you've changed, darling," Julia said, looking down at him. "You never used to worry about what other people thought."

"Julia, look, let's cut this short, okay? I'm a dying man. Just tell me what you want from me."

"Don't you know?" Julia laughed, undoing her long striped college-girl muffler and slipping out of her storm coat.

"And kindly keep your clothes on," George said. "I assure you all you'll get for your pains is a bad case of pneumonia. Double."

"Is that what you think you have this time?" Julia asked sympathetically. "Dear me, you really are in a bad way, aren't you? What's the matter, darling, has your love life been giving you so much trouble lately? . . . No," she added with a smile, familiarly placing herself on the couch with George's feet in her lap, "no, I can see from that menacing expression that I'd better stay out of your love life."

"All right," George said, raising himself up and perspiring with the effort. "So I exaggerated. So maybe I'm not actually dying. But I swear to you I really am sick as a dog—no, I take that back too, those beasts of yours will outlive me by a hundred years. Anyhow, Julia, I do have a lousy cold, in fact I'm so bleary-eyed at the moment I can hardly even see you sitting there on top of my *Selected Poems*. In short, I am in no shape for monkey business—"

"—oh, really, George."

"Nevertheless, if you feel that I owe you an apology right here and now, then I am prepared to apologize. If you truly feel that I've outraged your virtue, led you up the garden path—this I strongly doubt by the way, I have a nasty suspicion you led *me* there, but never mind, as a gentleman I concede the point—or wronged you irreparably or left you in the lurch, then I am most humbly and heartily sorry. I mean it. I'll give you back your curtains. I'll do anything but put it in writing. You have my solemn oath it will never happen again. All right? Now, please, Julia, if you have what you wanted, do me a favor and leave me in peace. But if you want to make love you'll have to find somebody else to service you. Because, god knows, sex with anybody is not on my mind at the moment."

"Except that I don't believe you," Julia said, calmly reaching for the bottle of bourbon and the shot glass lying on its side. "I thought we always agreed that sex was on everybody's mind all the time."

"Lay off."

"Oh, come on, George," Julia said pleasantly, "how about it? No one need ever know. To tell the truth I missed you."

"She missed me," George said in an oozy voice. "How do I go about convincing this woman it's really no dice?"

"But why? I'm just curious."

"You know goddamn well why."

"I don't."

"All right—I'm in love. There, does it make you feel nice and smug and superior to hear me say it?"

"No," Julia said, "actually it doesn't," and strolled over to the window where the two poodles on the porch were still straining and howling upward towards the early evening sky. She called down to them to stop, and when they went on, closed the window. "Oh, well, it's a shame though, isn't it? Especially since you still want me." She smiled as George turned over on his face. "Come on, George, I can tell you do. And don't bring up that cold again either, because I can remember a few afternoons when—all right, you can stop hiding. But it was so nice and pleasant with us before."

"It was an arrangement," George's muffled voice informed her. "It stank."

"No, we enjoyed each other. And now, just because—" She sighed and finished her drink. "Lord, what a dull town this is, especially in the winter. I'll be glad when spring comes and I can start gardening again."

"If you're thinking of leaving I'll stake you to carfare."

"Don't bother. All places are too much alike and so are all people."

"Dammit, Julia, doesn't anything get you where you live? Don't you believe in anything?"

"Of course I do. I believe in all the things you make fun of."

"Such as?"

"Oh, you know," Julia said reluctantly. "Having a home and family, putting down roots, security, being a good wife and mother—do you really want me to go into it?" She laughed. "Stop making such agonized faces. Even you can't deny that my husband and my children would be lost without me."

"You call that a loss?"

"What I *don't* believe in is baying at the moon when life can be nice and cozy."

"I detest coziness."

"Yes, that's what you say now, George. But like everyone else I've been watching you with this girl—"

"Whose guts you hate."

"—you're wrong, I rather like her. She likes me too."

"Keep away from her, Julia. I mean it."

"In a town this size? Don't be silly. Anyhow, as I was saying, I can see all the signs already. Today she has you falling on your celebrated backside. The obvious next step is marriage."

"You sound hopeful about it."

"Why not?" Julia smiled. "Maybe when you're all settled down and things aren't quite what you expected—who knows?—I might pay you another little visit."

"My god, you're an even worse bitch than I thought. Julia, go home and make supper for your husband. And take those poor suffering animals with you."

"All right," Julia said, ignoring the bitch part, "but you can understand that it's awfully hard to imagine you playing the faithful lover." She put on her heavy storm coat, pausing with the long striped muffler in her hands. "By the way, what makes you think she won't betray *you*?"

"Because, I regret to tell you, she's incapable of betraying anybody."

"Oh?" Julia said with an interested smile. "I was just wondering, you see, because she's alone with Seymour at the moment. In fact, she's been alone with him most of the afternoon."

"And so? What are you implying?"

"Nothing."

"But if there were something that would be just dandy with you?"

"I'm afraid," Julia shrugged with amusement, "that Seymour isn't quite as brave about these things as you are. Or used to be. But a little distraction—"

"Boy you really do have the soul of a pimp, don't you?" George said. "Julia, I mean it. Get the hell out of here and stay away from me. Far away!" and choking on the last word immediately broke into a violent fit of coughing.

"When we were little," Julia remarked, "we always used to say that the first one to get mad lost the argument. Except that we weren't having an argument, were we? Don't you want some water?" George picked up one of his galoshes and threw it at her, knocking over his vaporizing machine instead, which immediately began to gush oily water over his papers.

Julia gave him a long pitying kiss and slipped out the door. "Bitch, bitch—bitch!" George repeated, as the last of her footsteps and the horrendous barking of the dogs died away. "I never saw anything in you—*never.* . . ."

Gripping his head, he stared down into his lap, feeling even sicker about himself than before.

Obviously it was not going to be a night on which a man could take his rest. In the midst of a dream in which a fallen angel had brought him gifts in the moonlight, and was kissing his sweaty brow and telling him to eat something like a nice boy, George wearily groped for his light.

"Ah, yes," he said, after a moment, "—Campbell's chicken noodle, I see. How kind."

And as Daisy continued to stare at him in her thin white night-gown, stretching out her soup can with one hand, and holding a glossy brown fur coat so tightly together with the other that it tousled her blond curls in the back, he added, "But a little late in the day, perhaps?"

"Better late than never?" Daisy suggested, placing the little can on top of his bookcase where it stood red and uneasy next to a well-thumbed volume of Yeats. "Please, my darling, I wonder could we save all the symbolic reproaches until morning? I'm afraid I'm terribly sore in spirit tonight."

"And also body?"

"What's that supposed to mean?"

"It's a pun. I thought you liked them. It means where the hell were you all day?"

"Well, you said yourself not to follow you—"

George quickly reached down for his bourbon.

"—so what could I do but skate around by myself for a while, so as not to call attention to our little contretemps, as it were? And then when I finally did start home, I had this perfectly terrifying encounter with that awful Babbitt, Dudley and . . ." Daisy paused for a moment, thoughtfully righting the vaporizer that still lay across George's crowded work table, though it had long ago gushed itself dry.

"No, that's not fair, is it?" Daisy said. "In the book, Babbitt is really very nice."

"When you finish the literary criticism," George said, "I'd be curious to know where you spent the rest of the day."

"The rest of the day?" Daisy said, sitting down on the edge of the couch where George still lay with the Indian blanket muffling him to the ears. "—oh, why after that, I dropped in on the Lipshanskys," and gently tucked in his toes as she sat beside them, back stiff, rather like one of the Polish ladies at the tea, except that she was using George's feet as an armrest.

"The weather is really quite mild for this time of year," Daisy volunteered with a smile, after a pause. "Tomorrow it might do you good to get some fresh air. In moderate quantities, of course."

"How was Julia?"

"Julia?" Daisy repeated, offering him the box of Kleenex, to which George shook his head. ". . . Well, actually, I didn't see too much of *Julia*. In fact, I think Seymour mentioned something about she'd taken all the children to see Dr. Rust. Though you're perfectly right about that too, of course. I mean, it really is amazing, isn't it? One always thinks of Julia as a kind of all-embracing modern mother, and yet when one examines the situation closely—or rather, the children . . ."

"In other words," George said, padding out of bed in his pajamas to put a record on the phonograph, "you were *alone* with Seymour all afternoon. Is that correct?"

"If you want to put it that way."

"I do," George nodded. (*Cosi Fan Tutte—he* smiled to himself grimly.) "—and I imagine you talked a lot?"

"Well, yes."

"And I'll bet he told you all those poignant stories about his youth?"

"Yes."

"And?"

"I felt terribly sorry for him," Daisy said.

"*And?*"

"Oh, look here, my darling," Daisy said. "You know that I'm compulsively honest. Please don't ask me any more questions."

"So!" George cried, pointing a finger in her face with withering scorn. "While I lay here sick as a dog, you slept with that shmuck! Why not admit it?"

"Admit what?"

"—excuse me," George sighed, stopping to ease his damp flannel collar, "but could you please tell me how even *you* can laugh *now*, when the very sands of our life are shifting under us?"

"Because when you pointed that finger at me, you looked like Paul Muni playing Emile Zola."

"Where did you see it?"

"On the Late Show, over at Tootsie's."

"Daisy," George said, "I asked you a question before to which I now demand an answer. The simple truth will suffice. Did you, or did you not, let that creep Seymour Lipshansky make love to you today?"

"No," Daisy said staunchly. "I did not."

"So then why the hell are you crying now? What are you practicing to be, a pair of Greek masks?"

"I am *crying*," Daisy said, as the tears sprang into her blue eyes making them look like freshly watered flowers, "because I only have you on a heartbreaking technicality. And honesty, alas, compels me to tell you so."

"*Which* heartbreaking technicality?"

"—there was noise, as of children's laughter . . . footsteps . . . we thought—" She raised her eyes to him, and quickly dropped a heavy golden head on a very thin stem.

For a long while, George remained looming over her. Then rather to his surprise, he found that he had turned down the music and sunk down beside her, and was even nodding and numbly patting her little hand. Far in the background, soprano and tenor twisted and entwined in beautiful Mozartian filigree. But he and Daisy remained staring dismally ahead, he in his pajamas, she in her fur coat and nightgown, like two strangers in a doctor's waiting room.

". . . why did you do it," George said at last, slipping the coat off one of her shoulders and absently thumbing the soft bony young skin, "have you any idea?"

"You might also ask," Daisy said, with a racking sigh, "—why *didn't* I?"

"Because of course it's rather humiliating," George smiled, "as even you must understand." He shrugged. "I mean, if you had picked a handsome man, an intelligent man, even a minimally attractive man . . . but a spineless jerk like Seymour Lipshansky—?"

"It was a failure," Daisy nodded miserably. "But was it a failure in compassion, or should I just not have been there in the first place?"

"Go to hell."

"Oh, George, please," Daisy said, as the coat fell from her other shoulder. "I need you so desperately at this moment, please don't—"

"What *you* need is a psychiatric social worker. Maybe my wife can recommend one."

"But, darling, you know that I didn't want to tell you anything about this. You know that you forced it out of me. Don't you think you owe me—?"

"*Owe* you?" George cried. "*Owe* you! Listen, what form of self-deception are you practicing anyway? First you go prancing in and out of bed with any man you lay eyes on, but when you look up at *me* you're a plaintive virgin."

"George," Daisy murmured from the pillow, "I—"

"And then in your other incarnation, you're the pure young writer. Only now that I come to think of it, who the hell ever sees you writing a damn thing?"

"I've been emotionally tied up."

"In fact, who the hell even sees you reading a goddamn thing *I* write?"

"Don't you think," Daisy wept, "that perhaps some people live more by instinct than by education?"

"Only the part that kills me most, frankly—like a dagger in my heart, just in case that gives you any satisfaction—"

"Oh!" Daisy cried.

"—is that every word you say drops from your lips like a pearl of truth. And in the end it turns out that a filthy liar like Julia Lipshansky was right in the first place."

"What has Julia got to do with it? I mean, directly?"

"Don't change the subject."

"Oh, George, never mind the rest. Just take me in your arms and hold me tight, I implore you."

"Okay, I'm holding you. Now what do you want from me?"

"Marry me? End it all?"

"Oh, my god," George moaned, kissing her nose, her eyes, her sweet damp yellow hair, "don't you know yet, Daisy, that I wouldn't marry you if you were the last woman—girl—on earth? Why don't you just go on back home where you belong? You've come to this town with a theory and so far you've missed every single fact. Gorham is no place for you. You'll never survive here."

"But I love you!"

"No, my poor baby," George said, stripping the rest of her down as tenderly as he had their very first night and praying that he would never see anything so young and naked again, "I was never your lover—only your first big achievement."

12

THE HOUR EBBED SLOWLY AWAY, and the girls to whom she had given an impromptu composition to write as much to fill up the hour as on account of certain strained encounters with Professor Brooks, were still hard at it, bent over their desks in an agony of concentration, so that the silence in the classroom was thick and tangible like honey. Occasionally one of them looked up and frowned absently toward the small podium where Daisy sat chin in hand staring out at them, or another would twist a moist, pink, puzzled face around to the back of the room where the clock was hanging. But their eyes when they happened to meet anyone else's were quite sightless and impersonal, so that aside from the clock ticking away and the smooth scratch of ballpoint pens over paper and an occasional cough, there was nothing on anyone's part to disturb the peace. If peace, Daisy thought, contemplating one of George's favorite quotations about marriage (". . . from the hurly burly of the chaise longue to the deep, deep peace of the double bed . . .") was what you were looking for. Should she ask him where it came from? No, better not, since to all her questions this past week even perfectly civil ones like "Do you have any laundry?" or "And how is little Gary these days?" and "My god, even if we're not lovers, can't

we be friends?" he had given her no answer at all, except to the last—
"You don't want to be friends." And yesterday at the department meeting he had leaped to his feet to deliver an impassioned plea against shortening the required reading list and then calmly dozed off beside her while everyone else raised hands and voted (he had won, naturally), snoring away where another man, a normal man, would surely have been driven mad by the memory of her flesh. "Put, put, put," Seymour had said commiseratingly afterwards, "just like a goddamn motor-boat." Except that this was no help either since everywhere she went these days, home, school, coffee shop, there was Seymour popping up, her own overgrown sheepish version of original sin, even in the kitchen at the bring-your-own-bottle party Saturday night at the Pilsners' (yes, she had gone, what else could she have done?) where the rugs had been rolled up for dancing and the married couples had come separately to save on baby sitters.

"Seymour! What are you doing? Behind the refrigerator is no place to—"

"She can't see us. We're here in shifts."

With a difficult sigh, Daisy picked up the *Gorham Gazette* which she had brought along to while away the hour, and put it down again within two minutes having informed herself through its few pages of the arrival and departure of three mothers and two mothers-in-law (there was a slight mention of a Berlin crisis on the last page, but it did not seem very important). Several birds cooed contentedly in the snow beneath her window and she walked over to it, looking out idly over the rosy-tinted whiteness that made a perpetual Christmas card out of the entire campus, and reminding herself that it was the kind of scene that no one except George might object to, and that everyone else would merely sound like Henny Penny squawking that the sky was falling down.

In a few more minutes the bell would ring. Already the thin trickles of girls emerging from various buildings were swelling into a giggling, chattering series of streams crisscrossing in all directions. Were there more of them than there used to be, she wondered, or was it only the absence of other things that made them tend to leap out at her eye wherever she looked, like a newly learned word from a familiar page?

Coughing away in chapel, poking their sneakered toes in the small of her back at the movies. She craned her head more sharply downward. Somebody in the English department had released his class early and a whole fresh troop of girls was brushing past the withered ivy down below carrying along with them a short, painfully familiar figure muffled against the cold whom she regarded intently until not at all to her surprise he turned into the Dean of Admissions scurrying into the Administration Building. She looked away quickly. Oh god, it was beginning to be unnerving, this habit of seeing him everywhere, whether he happened to be there or not. Yesterday, she had even watched him emerge intact from the Science Building, where the real George Auerbach would surely have blown himself to bits with a Bunsen burner. Not that it was anything to worry about. It was merely the kind of illusion that people always suffered when someone they loved died. Died? But which one of us is dead, she wondered, absently staring down at the front row, where two freshmen immediately unlocked heads and glared back, mutely protesting their innocence. But had she accused them of anything? Daisy asked herself, compounding her own confusion. She returned to her desk and quickly told the class to finish up and start passing their papers down the aisles, using a brisk but friendly nod in the style of Gabrielle Hochmeister, who was a master of this type of gesture.

No, she must try to remember that she had nothing to put a finger on and complain of. On the contrary, her life this past week was what any reasonable person would opt for, or had opted for already, which amounted to the same thing. Up with the larks (she had long ago abandoned the idea of finding out what really cawed outside in the bushes), a brisk freezing walk over to the campus, several hours of classes, lunch at the faculty club surrounded by lace paper doilies and self-dripping candlesticks, back to the freshmen, a long, very long evening for work and meditation (which was what she had come for in the first place, wasn't it?) hair up, lights out all over town, and so to bed. If it should become too lonely, there was always the possibility of a little distraction. Maybe a few beers and a movie with Steve and Jeff, the painters, maybe a lunch, brunch, dinner, or any one of the things that Julia Lipshansky had begun to invite her to, always smiling inscrutably when Daisy refused as if though she did not particularly enjoy her own life, she always found other people's extremely amusing. Sooner or later, Daisy would accept, of course, even if it was only the lift over to the Amelia Lacey Memorial Ceremony. Who could grapple with a greased pole? (Although, ah what a temptation it was to hate that woman, which she would have done if she were not in Julia's debt, to the tune of one husband, to be exact, and whether Julia knew it or not.) And besides, it was pointless to go around creating difficulties. They were all trying to be nice, that was all—Seymour, Julia, the boys from the art department—even by an awful leap of the imagination, Edgar Dudley, who had advised her that morning that he was still deeply concerned with her future welfare. Nice, nice, nice, nice, nice. If Auerbach had been the Dark Continent, they could not have been nicer about welcoming her back at the airport.

"It's not a very rewarding topic, you know, Miss Lerner," Doris piped up from somewhere in the rear.

"What isn't?" Daisy said.

"What you just told us to write about. Do you think it's very rewarding, Miss Lerner?"

"Oh, *that*," Daisy said. "No, of course not. But apparently it's in the syllabus. In fact, I gather from the most unimpeachable sources that you were all supposed to have tackled it the first week of the term."

"Yes, we know that," Doris said. "But the first week of the term you said we should forget all about the syllabus and try our wings."

Had she really said that? She glanced at Doris darkly, and also at several other members of the class who had unconsciously begun to flap their elbows, feeling as if her old sins were coming back to roost on her, or worse, as if they had got hold of her baby pictures and were passing them around. But they were all so well-fed and earnest it was impossible to suspect them of anything, except maybe a simpleminded conspiracy to inherit the earth; and they were probably just following orders about that too.

"Yes," Daisy said finally, reaching under her desk for her briefcase. "Well, that's the way life is, isn't it?" She looked up. "I mean you start out with a set of aspirations, and then experience comes along and— whammo!—there you are in the sweaty grip of reality."

"Yes, Miss Lerner," Doris said, looking somewhat perplexed but very much subdued.

"In fact, you might even go so far as to say that it's the real tragedy of the human condition—this necessity to compromise—couldn't you?"

"Yes, Miss Lerner," Doris said, now subdued to extinction.

"You might even go further. You might even, from a metaphysical point of view, claim that without it man might soar to such heights that the *gods* themselves . . ." She paused. ". . . excuse me, but would you all mind not taking notes? Actually, this is the kind of thing you get right away or you don't."

As usual, they obeyed her much too readily, except for the ones who were taking notes about not taking notes, and had to be nudged into line. Then suddenly, there they were, row upon row of blank young faces staring up at her mournfully, like so many blobs of Silly Putty just released from their eggs. It was all very depressing. Didn't people like Professor Brooks who spent their lives molding young minds realize that they would let anybody stick a thumb in, and then just start oozing right out again?

Fortunately for all of them the bell rang, releasing everyone with a long shiver of electric current. There was a vigorous flurry of scooped-up notebooks, coats snatched from the backs of chairs, mufflers tossed around necks, and then they all trooped past her desk, inundating it with a flood of bluebooks. She attempted to pat them all into a tidy pile until, reminding herself it was her last class of the day, she shoveled them into the huge unappeasable maw of her briefcase. Then, having buttoned herself into her coat and secured a black hood over her hair, she stepped outside, gasping with the first icy smack of the wind against her face. Dusk was already glowering into evening (oh, why did even this remind her of him?) and all around her the campus was full of night sounds and night whisperings as the girls hurried off to their various dormitories full of suppressed excitement, like masked revelers on their way to the ball. Doris and Leslie too, on whom she suddenly took great pity, watching them mount their bikes with their coats open and huge bare knees exposed to the frosty air. There was still time to run across the road to the bookstore. Yes, the display of Amelia's *Poems* was still there—why had she thought it would vanish?—and after staring at it through the glass for a moment, she went inside and quickly bought a copy to stuff against a beating heart.

After the cold of the campus, Gabrielle Hochmeister's dormitory was very nice and warm, one of the few places evidently that Dudley bothered to heat. Also, although the food was all white, it came around on pretty plates with rosebuds on them. At the head of the beaming table which had been decorated with candles and russet winter flowers, Gabrielle sat smiling like a mother hen whose chicks had all hatched very nicely, especially one, a plump brunette with bangs and hair in a coil named Marcia who had been chattering all through dinner about the intricate details of her future, fluttering her left hand so that its diamond shattered the light into a thousand expensive splinters.

"So after Daddy popped an artery about the fishforks, and Mummy calmed him down, I said to Bob, 'Well, I certainly *am* going to make a studio out of the garage because if I can't express myself *after* marriage then I—'"

"Marcia's engaged," Gabrielle explained, beaming even harder so that she looked as if she had just finished combing her hair with an egg whisk.

"Yes," Daisy said, "so I gather."

"Only a little *papillon*—aren't you, Marcia?—but we'll miss her anyway." She tore her eyes away from the girl reluctantly and gave Daisy a sigh of simple contentment. "And so we have you here at last. Almost I had given up asking you, you know."

"Really, Gabrielle?"

"Oh, yes. But now tell me, how are things with you? No bad news or anything of that sort, I hope."

"Everything's wonderful," Daisy said.

"Really?" Gabrielle said, shaking her head skeptically. "Americans are amazing, aren't they?" she remarked, addressing herself to Miss Badger, the other faculty guest. "With them everything is wonderful. Mark my words, when disaster comes not one of them will be prepared."

Daisy looked up. It was a very arresting statement, made even more so by the fact that Miss Badger greeted it with a very bright smile, like a bird's, and that a moment or two later with an air of having taken herself by surprise, Gabrielle also began to bark with laughter. The girls followed suit. Were they all sharing a little private joke, then? It was very hard to tell, since Gabrielle had a strong Germanic tendency to laugh in the wrong places and go blank when everyone else was laughing, and Miss Badger had been smiling all along. Or maybe it was only part of the general air of good humor, which since it was Faculty Night was compounding itself all over the dining room so that because the girls were in skirts for a change and had freshly combed and barretted their hair the effect was a cross between a children's birthday party and Ye Gorham Inn on a Saturday night—but without any men or boys. Yes, it was definitely their absence that made it all so warm and cozy and though a few male teachers were actually present, they were more like Seymour than George, pale bespectacled thistles in a field of gently rippling young wheat.

"Come," Gabrielle said to Daisy, as everyone rose, "you and I will go back to my room for a while."

"You ought to have taken a little ice cream, you know," Miss Badger said, who had just finished spooning it up methodically. "Very delicious. And a bequest, you know. From a dear alumna now defunct. I knew her well."

"A bequest?"

"Oh, yes. All of the dormitories have them, small funds for those little extras. You know, ice cream, peanut brittle, damask napkins. Our girls never leave us, you see."

"Never?"

"I meant in spirit."

"I'll make you some coffee on the hot plate," Gabrielle said. "You'll see how convenient it is."

"Whereas I find," Miss Badger volunteered in the happy accents of one long acquainted with her own digestion, "that even a thimbleful after three P.M. keeps me awake all night. I toss and turn until dawn."

"Goodness, Miss Badger," Marcia said. "How awful for you!"

"Well, my dear, I'm afraid that when you reach my age, you will encounter the same problem. Often a little bicarbonate of soda helps. One level teaspoonful in a tumbler of water."

"It's really more a question of neurasthenic type than of age," Gabrielle said. "I had an aunt once who suffered in the same way, although she is many years dead already. She lived with us in Koenigsberg," she added, putting to rest any possible doubts about the matter. "A very cultured woman. French I learned at her knee."

"Now that's one language I never have been able to get the hang of," Miss Badger said.

"Naturally not. No American ever learns French properly. Take the nasals, for example, in a phrase such as '*Ou sont les neiges d'antan?*' Girls—*song, d'antang. . . .*" Gabrielle beat time in the air as the girls repeated the words dutifully, even dipping them in the sticky mucilage of Gabrielle's own accent. "You see? Impossible. It's all part of the American provincialism. . . . Well, à bientôt, Miss Badger. My best to Miss Jenkins. . . . And you, young ladies, back to work now, yes? You too, Marcia. And no dawdling in the lounge."

"Okay, Miss Hochmeister."

"Yes is a better word," Gabrielle smiled, adding as they walked down the hall and entered her room, "—Marcia's engaged."

"And you really don't get tired of having her say yes to you all the time?" Daisy said, sitting down in the same leatherette armchair where an hour before she had sipped at a shot glass of sherry.

"You prefer *okay?*" Gabrielle said with surprise, settling into its mate. ". . . ah, I see, the attitude, you mean. But why should she say no?"

"Because she's young. Because she ought to."

"Rebellion for its own sake?" Gabrielle smiled, switching on the lamp. "That no, I've never believed in it. I've seen too many things in my life smashed and broken that way—this is an excellent reading light, incidentally."

"Yes, I can imagine how you must miss all you've left behind."

"Connecticut College for Women? Well, yes, it was nice. But then all these places are nice."

"I meant—but no, look, what about the present? Do you really never stand in front of a room full of those girls and think, my god, does it always have to be a matter of pushing a peanut up a hill with your nose?"

"You'll never be a teacher if you think along those lines," Gabrielle said, shaking her head.

"I am one."

The two of them sighed and fell silent, each for her own reasons, though it was clear from the neat fold of her hands in a navy blue lap that Gabrielle had once been commended for her ability to sit still. Aside from her hair, which was wild and curly and through which her ears erupted, everything else about her was nice and tidy, including the blue serge dress which having made a stiff ascent over a pair of high haunches, collapsed altogether across the bosom. Also, although Gabrielle actually wore a few ornaments, a couple of bangle bracelets, a large ornate ring, a silver brooch with a dull yellow stone, it was impossible to imagine her actually putting them on before a mirror.

"Yes," Daisy said, "well, it's been a long day for everyone. I guess I'd better be getting on. But thank you for a lovely evening."

"But why so soon?" Gabrielle said. "We haven't had the coffee yet."

"Yes, I know, but I think I'd better save that for another time because I have a tremendous amount of work to do tonight and I—"

"Now, now," Gabrielle reminded her with a smile and an uplifted finger, "we all have work to do. Unless you're needing to make up for time spent on pleasure," Gabrielle added with a look of mock sternness before she threw back her head and laughed. "Only a little joke," she explained, composing herself again. "I haven't offended you?"

"No."

"And yet," Gabrielle remarked, cupping her chin in her hands and studying Daisy intently over the tips of her fingers, "how very sad you are. I've sensed it all evening."

"Sad?"

"You could tell me about it, you know."

"Tell you about what?"

"Everything?" Gabrielle suggested softly, while her eyes normally brown, suddenly became two black marbles fixed on Daisy avidly.

If she had studied the confidential approach by mail and missed the first two lessons, she could not have been clumsier. And yet, well wasn't it easy to see a girl like Marcia laying her head on Gabrielle's bosom and being soothed by the nice teachery smell of eau de cologne and cool linen?

"Listen, Gabrielle," Daisy said, leaning forward impulsively, "not that I mean to compare us—God knows you're one who's really suffered in your time—but what do you think it's earned you?"

"Suffered?" Gabrielle said, stiffening all over.

"You've gone through bloody hell. Your life has shrunk to the size of a small suitcase. You're a good generous person. But what I want to know is—what's your *protest*?"

"Metaphysics," Gabrielle murmured, standing up and dusting the chalk off her dark skirt, "I'm afraid I can't always dabble in them—not that I don't admire people who have the time."

She began making little adjustments about the room, fixing the set of a lamp here, wiping out a clean ashtray there, smoothing the pale blue coverlet on her bed. "Excellent mattress," she remarked, pressing it down with the heel of her hand, "no lumps anywhere. I don't think I've ever had a better one, even at Wheaton."

"You've taught at Wheaton too?"

"Like everyone else," Gabrielle said pointedly, "I go where I'm invited. But fortunately the dormitory life here is exceptionally pleasant. One somehow feels that nothing bad can ever happen—three full meals a day, a nice room, good companionship . . . It's a shame you can't have such a place also," Gabrielle smiled, patting Daisy on the cheek, "but you're such a little *papillon* yourself, I'm afraid you'd have trouble keeping the others in line—oh, must you really rush off? Then come, at least take a look at my bathroom before you go, otherwise you won't have seen the whole thing."

"*Voilà!*" Gabrielle said, opening the door and peering inside at the shining white tile with as much interest as if she had never seen it before either. "Very neat, no? This arrangement, I mean. You see, there's my ironing board, always set up for whenever I need it—handkerchiefs, of course, I paste against the mirror while they're still wet. And there on the shelf I keep my own private hot plate. It's small, but it heats up very quickly. I can make tea, coffee—soup also, though I don't care for it. So you see, I have everything I need right here."

Her eye traveling its pleasant course suddenly stopped short at a line of underwear drying over the bathtub. She frowned uneasily.

"*Everything*," Gabrielle repeated stubbornly, as if Daisy had denied it. But it was too late. The two of them stood there staring at Gabrielle's wet laundry as if they had opened a fish and exposed the wrong entrails. It was an amazing collection, though how Gabrielle had found the courage to shop for them in Gorham was a mystery: sheer black lace panties, red petticoats, tiny black brassieres with twin rosebuds neatly centered.

"Ah, Gabrielle," Daisy, almost bursting into tears. "So underneath it all—*ma semblable, ma soeur!*"

"*Semblable?*" Gabrielle repeated. She closed the door sharply behind her. "Do you enjoy mocking people?"

And then, being a refugee, she apologized at once.

That night as the woodpecker pecked away upstairs in fits and starts, it was very hard to work. She was even a little surprised and disappointed when she came home not to have found Seymour Lipshansky lying on her couch, telling her how sweet and easy life could be if only Daisy would let it. The last time, he had left his eyeglasses behind and she had tried them on, wondering if they would make her see things differently. And in a way they had. Her room became a glittering myopic version of everything she had known for months. Familiar objects had contracted. They were bright but manageable. A doll-sized place with doll-house furniture. Very sweet, very very tiny. . . . She had never understood Seymour as well as at that moment.

With a quick glance at the ceiling, Daisy wrenched her mind back to the typewriter and wrote steadily on for a few more minutes even though the words came staggering across the white page like little drugged mice—"*Once there was* xxa. . . . *Once there was a town* . . . xx,"—and further down several characters began to change their names or spell them backwards. It was almost fascinating. But when the hero (?) took an entire paragraph to get out of a chair, she gave up and went into the icy bathroom where she undressed very quickly and slipped on her new flannel nightgown before the cold could seep permanently into her bones. Then, feeling more and more like Miss Badger, Daisy padded back to her desk to put out the light. Overhead the silence was sudden, but absolute. It was only ten o'clock, but George's typewriter kept Gorham hours—he's sleeping now, those little red socks are peeping out of the blanket, his hand is slung across my pillow. With her finger on the light switch, she glanced once more at what she had written. A hideous parody of *The New Yorker*. No, worse, a message stuck in a bottle and washed away by the sea. It's trying to tell me something, Daisy thought, regarding her manuscript with a certain wistful tenderness, only I don't know what it is.

13

ACTUALLY, it had turned out to be a pleasant, pretty afternoon at the old cemetery. There was not a large crowd, only a good-sized gathering. A few people had brought umbrellas and some woman sank a heel into a mushy grave and bumped into a child who began to cry. But the weather had brightened since morning with a winter sun hung low for those whose habit it was to look to the sky for encouragement, so that many people were looking up and also slapping their hands together and burying their noses in the crooks of their elbows with such a spirit of sheepish good nature that they gave the effect of a final chorus in a musical comedy. In fact practically the entire cast had lined up, waiting for Stella the star to make her appearance: President and Mrs. Steel, cheerfully self-effacing as usual; the tall stringy proprietress of Ye Gorham Inn; the college chaplain, Reverend Goodson, blowing his nose in clerical anticipation of the coming event; Babs Pilsner and her husband Bill with the twins climbing over each other in a single stroller; Mr. and Mrs. Milton Goldfarb; Edgar Dudley, standing nearby as if he owned the place but was not sure he liked the way it was being run; the president of the Rotary club; a waitress from the coffee shop; the two mannish ladies of the bookstore; Miss Badger;

Gabrielle Hochmeister shepherding a large giddy group of under-graduates in tan camel's-hair coats and plaid Bermuda shorts; many of the Ladies of Gorham speaking to each other in hushed voices to make up for the disappointment of not being at an actual funeral; and also a very sober gentleman with a distinctly professional air, who turned out to be the local undertaker. Yes, the entire cast, including scores of supernumeraries, except for one blatantly missing member. But then, as Daisy told herself, pinioned to the outer edge by a Lipshansky on either side (they had come late, the car refused to start, Buddy had lost his pants), George would hardly have been the hero if you could get him to line up with the others. No, if he were observing the occasion at all, which was in itself doubtful, he had probably made himself comfortable at home with a good bottle of bourbon and his own Edition.

"See him?" Daisy said, suddenly aware that Julia was expecting an answer to that calm impersonal question of hers. "Well, yes, I *see* him—we still live in the same house—but if you mean by seeing him really seeing him then I guess I—"

"That's right, we heard about your having to move out for a while," Julia said sympathetically. "And on account of that friend of his too. What a shame."

"And what a place," Seymour said, rolling his eyes. "My god, they'll probably try to strip you of everything that isn't functional. They may even bolt you in there like the furniture. . . . Listen, how about getting up a petition or something?"

"—although your new friends tell us," Julia continued smoothly, appearing not to have heard him, "that there may be room for you in one of the dormitories in the fall."

"My new friends?"

"Oh, you know," Julia said. "Gabrielle Hochmeister and that crowd. Frankly, I was a little surprised. I thought maybe you might be thinking about going back to New York instead."

"New York? No, I'm not going back to New York."

"Awful place," Julia agreed, "so horribly messy and dirty," apparently unaware that from the mother of Buddy and the mistress of the house they had just left it was an incredible statement. "Also probably one of the worst places in the world to bring up children, wouldn't you say?"

"I don't have any children."

"Oh, I'm sorry," Julia laughed. "I keep thinking everyone is as domesticated as we are. Don't you, Seymour?"

"Yeah," Seymour said.

An end of the long striped muffler with which Julia had bound her head came loose, and Julia tossed it over her shoulder, imprisoning the few gray-blond wisps of hair that had managed to escape so that they could only flutter feebly against her imperturbable profile. Daisy gave her a short, sharp look, suddenly seized with an overwhelming desire to see Julia Lipshansky just once on Fifth Avenue in broad daylight walking along like a well-bred washerwoman. She would be on her way to the Spence Chapin rummage sale. She would be carrying a pair of shoes with cuban heels in a separate brown paper bag. A delectable vision, but a very fleeting one since the cool image of the present Julia on her home grounds immediately overpowered the other, especially when Julia waved gaily to Tootsie Goldfarb, who was standing a few yards away bundled up to the ears and so clearly suffering from a dry itch all over that she could hardly wave back.

"We offered him a lift too, you know," Julia remarked.

"Oh?"

"But he wouldn't come with us."

"No."

"Of course, he's so terribly aggressive and overanxious," Julia shrugged, bracketing George with poor Seymour and the poodles, "he burns himself out. I don't suppose anyone could actually live with him, do you?"

"Live with him?" Daisy said. "Well, it would all depend on—I mean, look, Julia, I hope you're not blaming him for anything that—"

"Blaming him?" Julia laughed. "Goodness, it's not my business to blame anyone, is it?"

Well, was it? Oh god, if she only knew, or maybe she did know and just didn't give a damn, which made it even worse. I shouldn't have come with them, Daisy thought, shifting miserably from one foot to the other on the frozen ground, I'm no good at this game, I'm not civilized enough, and then to her utter horror caught herself exchanging a conspiratorial glance with Seymour, who was wearing an oversized black Russian caracul cap that pressed down against the rims of his eyeglasses and made his ears flap sideways.

"Dammit, where is that horse?" Seymour said, looking around with more sang froid than she had ever given him credit for. "What's today, anyhow, Wednesday? Let's go down to the Bijou tonight."

"Good idea," Julia said. "This thing won't last long and you can come back and have dinner with us first."

"Oh, but I couldn't," Daisy said. "I sort of promised Miss Badger that—"

"*That* dike," Seymour said, as Miss Badger perhaps overhearing her name turned around and waved enthusiastically, "what do you want with her? . . . Okay, we'll go to the movies afterwards, then."

"Afterwards?" Daisy said. "Oh, but afterwards I promised myself I'd really get down to work."

"What kind of work?" Seymour said sullenly.

"I started a book. Didn't I tell you?"

"Oh, bull. It can wait."

"Gracious, Seymour," Julia protested with a laugh. "The girl can write a book if she wants to."

"She doesn't have to write it tonight. Anyhow, she goes with everyone else. We saw you the other night with those two fags from the art department."

Julia cocked her head at him indulgently. "Do go with him," she said to Daisy. "He'll be miserable if you don't. And really, I don't mind baby sitting at all."

"You mean go without you?" Daisy said. "Oh no, I wouldn't dream of it. It—it wouldn't be any fun without you."

"Yes, it will. It'll be loads of fun, won't it, Seymour? . . . Goodness, why is everyone looking at me so strangely? If you really want to know, I think it's one of those Odets pictures, and I know that you both think he's wonderful, but I can't stand him. He always makes life seem so *dreary.*"

For some reason Julia giggled on the word dreary. In fact, she had been giggling on such words all afternoon, as if in her mind they lumped Seymour and Daisy together.

* * *

But the ceremony was about to start. Dr. Rust's gleaming station wagon had drawn up to the very edge of the graveyard, and gradually everyone who had been chatting, looking around, and in general beating off the cold shuffled to some form of attention as Mrs. Brooks stepped out in full regalia, from the waist down an Arctic explorer, from the waist up an eminent Victorian. "Your future landlady," Seymour remarked, giving Daisy a gloomy poke in the ribs, while not too far away Tootsie Goldfarb exclaimed in a voice of wonder, "My god! This year she looks like Willie Howard giving a French lesson!" to which Milton sighed as usual and asked her if she could please try to be quiet. It was not a large graveyard, as graveyards went, but Stella Brooks clearly cherishing every inch of it managed to make a stately progress out of the short walk to the Lacey family plot, followed by the miniature entourage of Dr. Rust and her husband. The priestess approaching her temple. The princess graciously acknowledging what she assumed to be the homage of her villagers. The villagers closed ranks, leaving a respectful space between her and the semicircle that they had formed of themselves. Only the local undertaker in a navy blue coat and dark homburg remained aloof and businesslike, and it was hard to tell why he had come in the first place, since the graveyard was no longer in current use, unless he took a purely historical interest in such things. But obviously there had once been a time, perhaps even in his day, when the Laceys had been one of the first families in Gorham. There they were, proudly shut off from the rest of the dead by a high, fancy filigree fence, inside of which they all slept around a weather-beaten stone angel, with only a few discreet headstones to mark them off one from the other: Edwin Lacey, Fairfield Lacey, Edwina Lacey, Lacey Lacey (this was the tough one—what was it, male or female?) and of course with a barely decipherable name, dear Amelia, modest in death as she had been in life.

At a signal from Stella Brooks who was clutching a wreath, the Reverend Goodson bared his head and stepped forward to read a brief invocation, looking mildly surprised when he had finished that no one had coughed but himself. He put his hat on again, no doubt blaming the weather. Then two seniors who were wearing black coats trimmed with mink and black beanies and had gone without lipstick, recited a few original verses, sonnets they appeared to be, although Amelia Lacey herself had composed tiny epigrammatic poems of a much looser structure. A proud look from Mrs. Brooks, a very short introduction, and then the president of the Rotary Club, painfully careful of his syntax under the circumstances, delivered a short address on the theme that both the town of Gorham and its college would be impoverished without the rich tradition of the other and that the press of time alone prevented a fuller expression of this mutual esteem. He ended in a tangle of "that which's" and retired to enthusiastic applause. And now the time had come for Stella Brooks herself. Silently, thrusting an arm through some secret aperture in the cape, she pointed to the high grillwork door through which she would soon pass in solitary grandeur to deposit her wreath on Amelia Lacey's grave. "Friends," she began, "dear friends all—" in a voice not unlike Eleanor Roosevelt's ". . . *squawk bleat, squawk bleat. . . .*"

No, Daisy was no longer listening. It was getting colder by the minute and still Stella Brooks who had been going on for half an hour showed no signs of letting up, though her breath was congealing visibly in the frosty air. The audience remained pale and attentive, Seymour too, from the looks of him, although it was clear that he was not listening either. Unless that thigh rubbing against her had a mind of its own, which was also possible. It was soft like Seymour, it was warm like Seymour, it was insinuating like Seymour, but it was tough and sinewy and full of the boldness of youth. It pressed against her harder, suddenly filling her with all kinds of desires she would rather not have had at that moment. She edged away, horrified by her own excitement and despair. Then she bumped into Julia, and it was Julia of all people who saved her, with a slight smiling turn of the head, half puzzled, half amused. But what am I doing here? Daisy asked herself with a start. (Too late? the twiggy ground had given away beneath her, she was falling into the trap.) What am I doing in this never-never land? How did I come to be playing it so cozy with this pair? Have they advertised for a spinster friend of the family, and am I the pal no Lipshansky home can do without? How do I already know that the moment Julia sticks a hand into her soiled breast to fix the big safety pin that holds her brassiere together that it's time to leave the dishes and go? When the train whistle blows, why do I quiver for those poor children playing out on the tracks? And where would it all end? Would they go on forever, the two of them, squeezing her tighter and tighter between those little invitations and the little giggled questions and always Seymour's doleful eyes pleading for a nipple, a knee, a soft piece of skin anywhere as long as the wife's back was turned? Was this what had become of the proud Daisy Lerner? *Oh, George, George, where are you? I can't seem to go it alone.* At the thought of him, her insides turned wet and moist. Internal bleeding. But surely time would heal it. Time affected everything, even Gorham, even this little cemetery which had once been in the center of town and perhaps still thought it was. But would the dead care if they awakened suddenly and found that it had all moved on beyond them, horses, buggies and all, leaving them far behind with only a few smokestacks from the factories and a couple of Italian saloons for company? Or wouldn't the faces gathered around the graves look any different? George, unbend a little, make a compromise. You don't have to think of it as a defeat, there are those who might even consider it a triumph—mostly psychiatrists, though, she realized reluctantly, as a shadow passed across her face reflecting this tangent which was beckoning to her against her will. With an effort she dismissed it and turned shining blue eyes on the hills in the distance. I don't care. He must know I'm here. If he still loves me, he'll come and find me. *Find me, George, find me.*

"Oh, hi, George," Julia Lipshansky said, as if no miracle had come to pass.

"You're late," Seymour muttered peevishly. "We thought you'd never get here."

"Well, I'm here now," George said, "so what are you beefing about?"

"Oh, George," Daisy whispered. "I knew you'd come. I knew it in my heart."

George looked at her curiously. "I always come," he said, "except when I'm out of town, naturally."

"I've started a new book. I know you'll be glad to hear that."

"Did you? That's nice."

"I'm devoting myself to it utterly. I—what do you mean, out of town?"

"You'd better hurry," Julia said. "She's going into the last lap. I can tell."

"Hurry for what? What's he supposed to do?"

Several people, Gabrielle Hochmeister among them, had turned around and were shaking their heads. Julia lowered her voice. "He opens the gate for Stella Brooks so she can put the wreath on. He does it every year. It's part of the ceremony. Didn't you know that?"

"*George* participates in this farce?" Daisy said. "No, that's impossible."

"Well, he does."

"Not that I suppose you've read the poems," George pointed out with a ghastly smile, "only she *was* considered one of the greatest poets of her time—"

"But you covered that in your *introduction!*"

"Oh, can it," Seymour said consolingly, as George continued on through the crowd, "don't let him snow you. Even he has to earn his keep and he knows it."

She opened her mouth to answer him and closed it again, since incredible as it seemed, Stella Brooks actually was waiting for him, and as George shouldered his way through the tangled outer rim of the audience, caught his eye significantly, swelling and ballooning out like a homeward bound schooner.

". . . and so, in grateful memory of those *imperishable* gifts, I lay this wreath on her grave!" One octave lower. "George Auerbach, our Poet-in-Residence, will open the gate—George?"

Nodding, George yanked the rusty iron handle on the old gate. He yanked again, and then again. "Give me the key, Stella, it's locked."

"Key?" Mrs. Brooks said, wreath extended. "What key?"

"Try it again, George," Oscar Brooks said.

George tried it again. "It's either stuck or locked."

"There *was* a key," the local undertaker said, pursing his lips thoughtfully. "I know, because a few months back I was showing the lettering to some folks from Springfield. But who did I give it to?"

"Don't look at me," Edgar Dudley boomed. "Housing and Grounds isn't in charge of this piece of land." However, people were looking at him. "Ha, ha, ha," he laughed, to show he had just made a little joke. "Come on, George, give it a little more elbow grease."

With a disgusted glance at Dudley, George rammed his shoulder against the gate, as if he half expected it to yield suddenly and deposit him inside face down. He was mistaken. The thing refused to budge. "Anybody else care to try?" he asked, glancing around the crowd.

No one volunteered.

"Oh, Oscar!" Mrs. Brooks cried despairingly.

Oscar Brooks and George Auerbach caught each other's eye and nodded simultaneously. "Stella," George said, "have you ever played baseball?"

"As an adolescent. I was very athletic."

"Okay, sweetheart," George said. "Here's your chance, then. Go ahead and pitch."

In all fairness to Mrs. Brooks it had to be said that her wind-up was magnificent even though her delivery was a little wide of the mark. High in the air the wreath sailed, sending down a shower of laurel leaves and smaller carnations, and clearing the gate by a good two inches. The grave it landed on belonged to Lacey Lacey, the teaser, but everyone applauded just the same.

"Well," George said, "that's the ball game," and shook hands all around. Mrs. Brooks, so flustered and happy that in the heat of the moment her red fox collar had fallen open to reveal her binoculars, paused in the midst of all the congratulations to give herself a hard slap in the eye.

"What is it, my dear?" Oscar Brooks said. "Headache?"

"What? No, dearest, something seems to have splattered me."

"*Splattered* her?" Tootsie Goldfarb's bright laugh rang out in the sudden unfortunate silence. "I thought for the rich they *sing*." Equally distinctly, Milton was heard to ask her to please shut up for once in her life and Tootsie, who was still smiling juicily, burst into tears, so that Milton had to put his arm around her. "You see?" Babs exclaimed to her husband. "I told you Tootsie was pregnant again. It was the only solution." Everyone began to mill around quickly, sending up an awkward babble of good-byes.

"Look, Julia, I'll say good-bye now too. Good-bye, Seymour."

"Hey, wait a minute. Where are you going? Don't you want a lift back?"

"No, no, please, Seymour, I have to be by myself for a while."

"But what about the movies?"

"I don't know. I'll call you . . . okay, I'll meet you when I get through with Miss Badger—no, I'm not through with Miss Badger already . . . Oh, I'm sorry, Mr. Dudley—Edgar—I didn't see you . . . No, thanks a lot but I really couldn't. I just explained to the Lipshanskys too, I'd rather walk—"

"You can always walk," Edgar Dudley said. "Come on, little lady, you and I have business together."

Daisy opened her mouth and screamed.

"Oh, for christ's sake," Edgar Dudley said, "what the hell's the matter with you now? What do you always have to fly off the handle for?"

"That *bird* over there!" she wept, clapping a hand to her heart. "It made a face at me. I think it was a *raven!*"

"There are no ravens around here," Edgar Dudley said, without even looking around. "This is a clean, well-kept place. Come on, before you get all the other females hysterical."

"Undoubtedly a small crow," Gabrielle Hochmeister agreed. "Americans never know what to make of them."

Why were they all so calm, Daisy wondered, trying to stop crying. Was she only seeing things again? And with her record, could she insist that—no, there it went! A medium-sized, rather fat black bird. It blinked at her once or twice, gave her a toothless smile, and minced sedately off between the tombstones. George! Where was *George?* George was there and not too far away either, with his collar turned up and a peculiar, almost sorrowful look on his face. Stella and Oscar Brooks were calling to him, and he shoved a beret on his head and walked away.

14

LIKE ALL ESSENTIALLY ROBUST PEOPLE, when Mrs. Brooks fell ill she tended to fold up like an accordion, which was precisely what she did a few days later, including the soft little discordant moans when the last of the air went out of her. It was that sudden. One minute she was laughing over the telephone to Sue Carp, still savoring her triumph at the cemetery, the next minute she was struggling to reach a chair. By the time Oscar Brooks got her to bed, she was running a temperature of 104 and retching over the side. Also her head ached so, that she kept touching it with a kind of feverish incredulity and whimpering "Oscar, Oscar" while her glazed eyes failed to perceive that he was right beside her, as he had always been.

Professor Brooks had never before considered himself a helpless man—a little too courtly perhaps, yes he knew that, and sometimes stiffer than he meant to be, but certainly always at his best with ladies in distress. And to see such distress, and the lady his wife, and to realize that there was practically nothing he could do for her, had taken the starch right out of him. He was even limper after Dr. Rust paid his first visit and left with a hurried promise to return in the morning. "Oh, my dear, oh my very dear," he murmured, wiping off her face with a damp cloth and feeling the fever burn through it. Then he began to rub her wrists with alcohol, and smooth her lank hair, and fix the set of her pillow, aware that he was accomplishing very little, until he finally stopped to catch his breath and wipe his own forehead.

He had closed the high narrow windows for fear of drafts and by now the air in the bedroom was stifling, so that on account of the nautical nature of the furniture—the twin bunks attached to the walls with rigid chains, and the tables riveted to the floor—Oscar Brooks felt vaguely like a stowaway deep in the hold of a ship, especially with poor Stella pitching back and forth in constant danger of falling out of her berth. Oh, what a fool he had been to let that arrogant ass of an architect bully him into this arrangement. But then poor Stella too had been so enthusiastic about the plans—he could see her now, almost prancing in her eagerness to see them realized—that no one could have predicted the time when he would have her shoved away up there like a sailor's bundle. Oh, how wrong it all was. Why, Stella ill should have a big fourposter bed with cushions and flowered quilts and a warm yellow sun to stream in on her. Stella ill—but how was this possible when Stella had never been ill before? By god, if she recovered, no *when* she recovered—Dr. Rust had sworn she would—he would make it up to her. How, he was not sure, and it did not matter anyway, since in the midst of trying to comfort himself—"Hush, Stella, hush, my darling . . ."—he dozed off, and when he awoke it was to hold a basin to his wife in a disinterested gray dawn. He looked at her face. All the symptoms that Dr. Rust had mentioned had appeared while he was sleeping.

"But are you certain that's what it is?" Oscar Brooks whispered, following Dr. Rust limply out of the bedroom and closing the door part way behind him.

"Not yet. But you saw her."

"But it's impossible. This kind of thing just doesn't happen."

"It happens all the time, Oscar, only laymen never pay any attention. Why, just last year in Texas—"

"Texas?" Professor Brooks repeated with something of his old spirit. "—I was hardly referring to Texas."

"Well, apparently it's happened in Gorham too," Dr. Rust said, perhaps a little more curtly than he intended since Oscar Brooks began to wilt again and needed a strong hand to steady him. "And the sooner we appreciate that fact, Oscar, the better."

"Appreciate?" Oscar Brooks said hollowly.

"Look here, do you have anything strong in the house?"

"Can she have it?"

"Not for her. For you."

"Just the sherry."

"Well, take some. I'll get you some Miltown too."

"Oh, William," Oscar Brooks said, shaking his head. "I don't need anything at all. All I want is for her to get well—she *will* get well, won't she?"

"I have her on penicillin. If that doesn't do the trick, we'll put her on chlortetracyline. . . . Come on, Oscar, don't look so stricken. We'll have her as good as new in a few weeks. And you're not going to be much help if you fall apart."

"But it's such an insult to her," Oscar Brooks said. "And you know her, William, so delicate in spirit, so . . . she doesn't deserve it, she—"

The telephone rang. As Professor Brooks went to answer it, leaving Dr. Rust with a series of complicated instructions about how to heat a simple cup of coffee on the modern stove in the kitchen, Dr. Rust took out his pipe.

". . . yes, yes, of course, I'll certainly tell her you called. Thank you so much for inquiring . . ."

"Has there been a lot of that?" Dr. Rust asked.

"Well, everyone wants to know how she is. This time it was Edgar."

Their eyes met unwillingly and they both looked quickly away. "I think I hear her," Oscar Brooks said, cocking his head. "I think she wants something."

They tiptoed into the bedroom. Stella Brooks was turning her head fretfully back and forth and murmuring, "Oscar . . . *Oscar!* . . ."

"I'm here, darling, I'm always here." He leaned closer.

"What does she want?" Dr. Rust said.

"I'm not sure . . . it's something about Amelia—that Amelia Lacey is Jewish. . . . Actually, she's been saying it over and over . . . I tell you, William, I—"

"All right, get hold of yourself," Dr. Rust said. "We have more important problems to consider right now."

Oscar Brooks raised his head. Once more they engaged in that brief meeting of the eyes that was so painful to them both. Dr. Rust took up Stella Brooks' wrist, glancing at his watch.

"Now don't you worry about anything," he said with a distinctly professional air. "You just leave the worrying to Oscar and me."

"For goodness sake, stop crying," Julia Lipshansky said, who had always loathed the sight of a man in tears. "Why do you always have to cry after—"

"I'm not crying," Seymour said, sniffling peevishly. "I told you before, I think I caught something the other day. It's a shame too. I was going to work this afternoon."

"You didn't catch anything."

"Well, Stella Brooks is sick," Seymour said, raising his head from the pillow with such an aggrieved look that Julia shrugged—which appeared to grieve him even more—and lay back again beside him.

Reminding herself to telephone Mrs. Brooks later on, she reached into the pocket of her bathrobe for a cigarette, and remembered as her fingers fumbled among stale tobacco crumbs that there were no more in the house. Not that it really mattered, she was hardly a serious smoker, but nevertheless an annoying sense of prickliness and irritation came over her. Or maybe it was all those awkward interruptions by the children, who had come peeping in at the door, goggle-eyed, all four of them, and at exactly the wrong times—except that neither she nor Seymour paid any attention when *that* happened anymore, they were so used to it. No, it was probably just the impending snow that made the room so dark even at this early hour and filled the atmosphere with that curiously uneasy electricity. It was always so hard to remember in the summer how long winter could last. And where had Buddy's sled managed to hide itself this time? The last she remembered seeing of it was during the sudden thaw a few weeks ago, poking up its runners between the rusty cans and the old snow-covered spare tire on the other side of the flower bed. Had she dragged it down to the basement then, or had the next snowfall covered it up again? Oh well, if Buddy came back she could always send him off to make a snowman, or if he was still blue with the cold, tell the other children to get him something to eat, though what there was in the house she had no idea since they had been ransacking cupboards all day. Somebody ought to clean up this mess, Julia thought, regarding the clothes scattered over the floor and the disheveled drawers with a certain weary detachment.

"Oh yes," she said, "I forgot to tell you. We don't have enough money for the rest of the month."

"We don't? But I thought . . ."

"You'll have to write to your father again."

"Aw, come on, Julia," Seymour protested, although as usual her silent stare ended the argument before it began. He raised his hand to wipe his eyes again, but with a glance at Julia thought better of it, and reached over to the covered orange crate that was the night table and busied himself blowing on his glasses.

"I don't understand what he ever saw in her, do you?" he said finally.

"Don't you?"

"Julia, please, don't start that again."

"You have it wrong," Julia said. "*I* haven't started anything."

"Julia," he beseeched her. "How can you after we just—"

"Well, obviously if you can lie to me about enjoying a movie when you never even went near the place," Julia said, "you can lie about anything."

"But we did go near it," Seymour insisted, "that's the point. Only I knew you'd leap to the wrong conclusions if I told you the truth in the first place and that's why I—Julia, don't look at me like that. Have a little faith in me, for god's sake."

"All right," Julia said, as Seymour turned over on his stomach and buried his face in the torn pillowcase. "Let's forget about it. Just don't start crying again."

"That snotty bitch," Seymour said in a muffled voice. "With that fancy talk and those fancy airs. And always throwing that book in your face. Big deal. As if anybody who wanted to, couldn't—"

"Did she tell you what it was about?"

ANN BIRSTEIN

"Her book? Who the hell cares. I got the feeling maybe it was about Gorham."

"Does that mean we're all in it?"

"I just told you. I don't give a damn."

"But I do," Julia said. "A lot of people will."

"Do you think so?" Seymour said, turning over.

"It's very possible. People don't like to be made fools of."

"A real hatchet job, maybe?" Seymour said interestedly, raising himself on one elbow. "It wouldn't surprise me after the other night."

"I told you I didn't want to hear about the other night anymore."

"Well, it wasn't *my* fault," Seymour said. "How did *I* know she was going to act like that? Making me cool my ass off in front of that movie house waiting for her. And then when her highness finally does show up, she won't even go inside because it's the middle of the picture and only Virgil can plunge into a story *in medias res* and come up with the sequence intact—or some shit like that—and how about some coffee first? You think I wanted to have coffee with her? All I wanted to do was see the picture and come straight home like you told me. But no, I have to sit there listening to her yak about graves and ravens and that lousy book and how resurrections only take place in the spring, and all the time she's got her face so covered up with that spooky black hood everybody's looking at us. And then, when I finally get her out and we both have our coffees paid up and we're back at the theater . . . boom, she's off on her high horse again. And if you think to this day I know why she—"

"Don't you?"

"That's what I'm trying to *tell* you," Seymour said testily. "Then the next thing I know, there we are in front of the box office, and I step aside so she can pay her seventy cents first, and she looks up at me suddenly and says, 'Maybe you'd like me to pay for you too?' So you know, what the hell, I kind of smile and say, well if she has *that* much change . . . And then she gives me a really wild look and starts to run like hell down the street."

"Shut up, Seymour."

"But who the hell does she think she *is*?" Seymour insisted. "Leaving me standing there like a bloody ass with those two tickets in my hand. Who the hell even wanted her fucking extra ticket? Oh, shit, I hope she croaks."

"Seymour—"

"Well, I do!" Seymour cried. "Goddammit, the great themes have been handled already. What entitles *her* to leave people standing there?"

"Stop crying," Julia said automatically.

"I'm not crying."

"You are."

"Yeah? Well, how would you like it if it happened to you?"

"It did."

Seymour had propped himself on one elbow to stare at her.

"You're my husband," Julia said, closing her eyes.

Well, she had set him off again, there was no doubt about that. The bedsprings creaked and groaned, and then he was blubbering away on her breast, his tears soaking through her soggy bathrobe to the naked skin beneath it. A fastidious tremor of revulsion passed through her. How strange life was. So much had already soiled this robe over the years: soft-boiled eggs, baby formula, urine, she hardly knew what else, and always these heavy wet tears were the only things that ever sickened her. The irony of it made Julia smile. When Seymour lifted his head questioningly, she paused a moment and then still smiling began to stroke his thin pale hair. A very awkward gesture, but it must have soothed him, since presently Seymour gave his little grunt and fell asleep.

It was hardly the first evening call that Dr. Rust had paid on George Auerbach and Dr. Rust certainly assumed that it would not be his last since he had considered himself a distant, but fond enough friend of George's for many years. Whenever George felt a sore throat or sinus attack coming on, he took it over to Dr. Rust's office in the Infirmary, and in return because he did not like to separate his professional and private life if it could be avoided, Dr. Rust sometimes invited George to a family musicale where George, who had been forced to study the clarinet as a child, tootled away happily as if the instrument had been his own idea in the first place. But obviously, George had never imagined that he and Dr. Rust would one day be sitting around discussing what they were discussing. Neither, for that matter, had Dr. Rust, though Dr. Rust was certainly taking it more routinely.

"Well, I'll be damned," George said, not for the first time that evening, caught between shock and laughter, and poured himself a stiff shot of bourbon, also not for the first time. "But, my god, William, how can you be so intellectual about it?"

"Well, you know how it is," Dr. Rust said, with a gratified tweak at his trousers, "it's my business, you might say."

"Still—"

"And then again, what's to be gained from being overemotional? Fortunately, it's an ornithological disease, and not communicable from man to man, so we don't have that to worry about. But of course, from the point of view of infestation—"

"Please," George said, "spare me the gory details."

This time it was Dr. Rust who laughed. "Why is it always the literary people who shy away from the simple facts of illness, I wonder?"

"Meaning me?"

"Meaning you," Dr. Rust nodded and smiled, "meaning Oscar, and how the idea—well, I suppose we just have to ascribe it to an overemphasis on symbolism in our culture these days. Still, George, maybe we'd better keep in mind that, factually speaking, until we can pinpoint the source, the less said of all this the better."

"But you know the source."

"Only in a general sense," Dr. Rust reminded him. "If Stella owned a parakeet or something of that sort, yes, we could nail it down right there. All it takes, you know, is intimate contact with a diseased feather or two, or better yet, some droppings—"

"Droppings," George repeated, reaching for another drink.

"But as it is," Dr. Rust concluded, politely waiting for George to swallow, "Stella's a bird watcher, and almost anything that's been flying around town that she might have come into contact with—well, you can see the problem."

George shuddered. "How is Oscar taking it?"

"Badly. He said it was an insult to Stella."

"It is."

"And also an extremely embarrassing situation for both the town and the college. Which is why—for that and many other reasons—it will be best to keep this as quiet as possible."

"Can you?"

"If everyone cooperates."

"Oh, they will," George said. "Don't worry about that. Cooperation is Gorham's middle name."

"Will you?"

"Will I? Now, don't try to bring *me* into this. What the hell do I know about it?"

"Perhaps if I presented you with a book on the subject?" Dr. Rust suggested with a wry smile.

"Okay," George said. "Touché, and all that. . . . But I still can't . . . I mean when I think of that silly ass decanting her S.S. Pierce bottle of sherry. . . . All right, don't look so worried, Willie, I promise to keep my mouth shut for a change, okay?"

Dr. Rust shook his head as at a naughty boy and laughed, and then the two men fell silent, as they often had on other occasions when the streams of their thought parted company. Actually, for the moment Dr. Rust was concerned with nothing more complicated than the fact that he was exceedingly tired, even wearier than during that terrible polio epidemic some years before, and that very soon he would have to bundle himself up and go back out into the bitter cold to see his patient. It would have been a much greater pleasure to stay in George Auerbach's cozy littered room and continue on to such topics as books and music, which they could have discussed in a nice contemplative man-to-man fashion. Not that George seemed to be thinking along those lines. He had sunk down into his armchair, poor man, and was looking around at his various medications as if his mind were suggesting so many possible symptoms that it depressed him even to think of choosing among them. It was a very familiar syndrome with George, and one that Dr. Rust had observed many times before.

"No, hey wait a minute—" George said suddenly, "—why me? Why tell me about it?"

"I thought you'd be interested. Aren't you?"

"William, what's really going on around here?"

"Nothing except what I told you," Dr. Rust said, "of which the less said the better, as I thought we both agreed. And which also means, naturally, that we'll want everything to proceed as calmly and normally as possible—"

"Well, yes, of course, but—"

"—including the arrangements for your friend, Atkinson."

"Christ," George said, "I forgot all about him. But he's not the type who'll—"

"—and therefore, since the girl is scheduled to move in a few days, by which time Stella will be well on the mend—"

"Which girl?"

Dr. Rust did not answer.

"Are you mad? Do you mean to tell me you're willing to let her march right into that place without warning her?"

"Warning her about what?"

"The danger, of course."

"There is none."

"Sure, that's what *you* say, William."

"Oh?" Dr. Rust murmured, neatly extracting a handkerchief from his tweed pocket and wiping his hands, "I didn't realize you were better qualified to say otherwise," and taking a quiet sip from the glass George had handed him earlier, began to leaf interestedly through a copy of a new quarterly on the table beside him while George stared. "Yes," he said finally, closing the magazine and looking around, "I wish I had time to keep up with all these things the way you do. You have a nice life here, George. Gorham's been good to you."

"Invidious argument. If you're trying to threaten me that way, forget it. It's pure McCarthyism."

"Oh, I'm not threatening you," Dr. Rust laughed. "How could I? I'm more like a man who's just handed you a loaded revolver and begged you not to shoot it." His face sobered. "And I know that you're responsible enough not to."

"In other words, I'm the weak link in your chain. You've tested all the others, and if I don't tell her no one else will."

"I haven't tested anyone—good lord, man, why do you insist on being so dramatic about this?—but if I did, I imagine you'd be the strong link. Why shouldn't you? Gorham *has* been good for you over the years."

"I've been good for Gorham."

"Precisely. It's been a mutually satisfactory arrangement."

"I'm asking myself if it still is."

"Now, George, please don't throw out the baby with the bath water. It's uncharacteristic of you, and really, if I may say so, unworthy. Besides, what could you possibly hope to gain from it? The loss of your privacy, your peace, your solitude, all of which your work depends on? Frankly, I doubt that you can even think of a better place than this to expend your creative energy, a place where you'd find a keener recognition of your status as a poet or, well, yes—more freedom to maintain it. Naturally, George, I don't intend to insult you by mentioning such matters as financial security, or the fact that you've always been very liberal in your criticism of the hand that feeds you and that no one has ever—"

"Can the crap," George said. "Somebody's got to tell her."

"Well," Dr. Rust shrugged, "you know the girl better than I do. It's perfectly possible that in spite of the fact that she seems to be writing some sort of exposé of us all, she's capable of a lot more discretion than I give her credit for."

"And cut out that exposé baloney too."

"I take it you've read this book, then?" Dr. Rust said, and when George failed to answer, "In any case, I'm not talking about her *rights*, George, no one's questioning them, no one's stopping her—this isn't Peyton Place, after all. I'm talking about—what shall I call them?—the nature of her perceptions. Come on, be honest with me. You're a literary man yourself. You also know this girl intimately—"

"Stop calling her 'this girl.' You know her name as well as I do."

"That's hardly the point. The point is, how would she be likely to handle the information I just gave you? Keep it to herself, take it in her stride? Behave in a manner that would benefit the community? Or run through the streets crying that disease was nesting in our trees and shrubs? Don't bother to answer. I can see the answer in your face."

"She has no reason to be loyal to Gorham," George said. "Also, from what you tell me, disease *is* nesting in our pretty trees and shrubs."

"In your enthusiasm for the metaphor," Dr. Rust sighed, "you seem to keep forgetting that we have now developed excellent antibiotics. Stella Brooks happens to be responding to treatment very nicely."

"All right, then just tell me this—would you let anyone *you* love walk into that house?"

"Someone I love?"

"And don't split hairs with me."

"Well, I was there at three and at five," Dr. Rust shrugged. "I'm going back at seven."

"Oh, for christ's sake, William," George said. "Nevertheless, you and Oscar don't really think, do you, that I'll sit here while—?" He had been pacing up and down like a caged tiger, only now in spite of what he had just said, he did sit down, shaking his head over and over again.

"Listen—she saw a *raven*," George said, almost pleadingly.

"Come now, George," Dr. Rust said, lighting his pipe and allowing himself his first flicker of impatience of the evening.

She had almost finished packing. She had always been a terrible packer as well as a hopeless arranger of objects in general—for example there were those Lautrec prints still gathering dust under the hammer—and so she had been at it for several days, hauling bags down from the attic, making lists, wondering if this might not be a good opportunity to give things away, and stopping to jot down a phrase or two that might come in handy later. It was a time when even Daisy could not call herself happy, but she was busy, which helped considerably, and all around her in that otherwise bare and grudging living room her steamer trunk and her suitcases were open and beautifully overflowing, like the cornucopias she still believed life could be. Brassieres, petticoats, frilly panties, pearls, stockings, a flame-colored chiffon evening dress, pointy red slippers to match—where had she expected to wear them all? She reminded herself that Edgar Dudley would be coming by for the heavy bags this afternoon and that the bus he had told her to catch would be leaving Main Street in half an hour and wondered who would ever know that she had lived in this place once she had closed the lids? The answer coming as a sharp imperious rap on the door stiffened her instantly into the shape of a startled faun.

An attitude in which George, having repeated his knock several times, barged in on her, kicking the door to with his foot. She had never had the slightest doubt who it would be. In all these months in Gorham George was the only person who ever knocked before entering, even when as now, he only stood there and glowered at her right afterwards.

And yet it was hard to believe that he was real, he was looking so exactly as she had once dreamed he would, as if the houselights had dimmed and only George remained in his own pool of light: his forefinger upraised, his mouth working futilely, rather like a carp's, his rounded shoulders burdened, his hair very gray, startlingly gray, even grayer than she had remembered, almost pure white at the temples, his brown tweed suit crumpled, disheveled, clearly slept in. And there was even—oh, the pain of it!—an old yellow copy of *Partisan Review* climbing out of his pocket.

Daisy turned quickly away to her desk. That *Partisan Review* had been a little too much. It was the same issue she had once carried around for weeks, hoping against hope that she would work up an interest in it.

Well, George thought, as he quietly lowered the arm which had been pointing like a prosecuting attorney's and reminding himself that he would have to consult William Rust tomorrow about that old bursitis in the left shoulder, evidently it was all going to be a lot easier than he had feared. A great consolation and enormous relief, of course, to a man who had arrived in a state of mental anguish, and yet in some vague disquieting way, disappointing. But though this meager, cottagy room was just as he had left it (and what had made him suppose George Auerbach's absence would make such a difference?) and the same old drafts still played dangerously around the bare windows, and the same old empty refrigerator chirped away in its usual mild agony in the kitchen, there was already a subtle change in the atmosphere. Maybe only on account of the steamer trunk in the middle of the floor with its suggestion of a great voyage, or the little traveling case into which after politely inquiring about his health and begging him to take a seat, Daisy was now busy shoveling the contents of her desk, including a silver inkwell, a crystal bud vase, a stapler, and also the yellow plume pen that always used to stand next to her type-writer. Yes, a definite relief, George repeated to himself, sitting down on the maple sofa and absently taking a sip from the can of beer Daisy had given him (her last apparently, since she was not drink-ing any herself), and crumpling aside an almost empty package of cigarettes (had she forgotten so soon he had stopped smoking?), a great relief to see her so calm. No accusations, though god knew he had braced himself for them, no scenes, not even in fact any ques-tions about why he had come, though he had phrased and rephrased the sentence all night long: "Now before you get any funny ideas, my girl, a few words of advice and caution . . ." Well, it was better this way, never mind about the disappointment. Better, far better than that she should have greeted him at the door and clasped those two slender white arms so tightly around a man's neck, he would have to kick, wrench, scream, yell, anything to keep from submerg-ing and drowning. In the midst of treading water, and feeling the green pounding rush of it against his ears, George paused a moment to pick up a piece of typing paper that had come fluttering down from her desk. So perhaps, he thought, glancing at the sheet before he handed it back, perhaps even Daisy Lerner had learned discretion at last, perhaps even *she* understood now that to survive in the world meant—he looked at the paper again.

"*Your book*," George said in a voice turned to stone.

"I beg your pardon?" Daisy said, raising a pair of very reluctant blue eyes.

"Your book," George repeated. "The one I assume that you've now told the entire world you're devoting yourself to utterly? . . ."

And without waiting for an answer, he read out loud: "*Once there was a town that loved itself so dearly every inch of it was precious to itself . . .*"

His voice petered out into silence.

"Excuse me," Daisy said at last, "I realize that there are too many *it's* in that sentence, but don't you think your reaction is a little exagger-ated—even from a literary point of view?"

"And may I ask," George said, very slowly and painfully, "why you have chosen to write about Gorham at this moment?"

"Gorham?"

"Is it about someplace else then?"

"Well, one could say, couldn't one, that every artist takes his own experience as a point of departure but that subsequently there is a transmogrification into . . . ?" She took the paper back.

"Anyhow, *you* were the one who told me to write about Gorham in the first place."

"And do you always do what people tell you? Who the hell are you, Dolly Dimple?"

"George, if you have come here merely to shout at me as in the old days, I must make clear—"

"*Shout* at you?" George shouted. "Listen, are you out of your mind to think that you can sit here writing about them and that they'll love you for it?"

"They were never supposed to love me for it," Daisy said, closing her desk drawer and snapping the clasps of her traveling case shut. She got up and went to sit on a suitcase lid or two, stuffing their contents beneath her, and finally brought together the two halves of the trunk as if she were entombing some vibrant form of life between them.

"I also told you a lot of other things which you seem to have conveniently forgotten," George said, "such as the suggestion that you take the next train back to New York, where you belong. Why didn't you do that?"

"Because there is such a thing as courage, Mr. Auerbach."

"Oh, what the hell does courage mean these days, especially for a woman?"

"I also felt I no longer belonged there, but here."

"Which are Julia Lipshansky's exact words on the subject, in case you're interested."

"Ah, yes," Daisy said, "so we're back to her again. Yes, I might have known."

"Known what? . . . Listen, where are you going with that suitcase? Put your coat down. . . . Don't you even want me to explain why I'm here in the first place?"

"Explain?" Daisy said over her shoulder with a heartbroken smile. "Oh, there's no need to explain. Not that I blame you for trying. Why shouldn't you have your own little academic version of *Back Street* like everyone else?"

"You forget," George said coldly, "that I'm not as familiar with the Late Show as you are. Also, what the hell are you talking about?"

"It's funny, isn't it," Daisy said, clutching her coat to her breast as she paused for a moment at the window, "how a thing will suddenly click in your mind? Just like a murder mystery. Take the clue of the unraveling curtains, for example. Two sets in two different houses. Yet both of identical material. Both left unhemmed by the same loving hand. Or was it the dogs barking at strange hours? Or the curious shadow plays behind drawn window shades? . . . Poor George. Auerbach the Great. Auerbach the Inimitable. Auerbach the Greek Chorus. And in the end it turns out Auerbach has the soul of the Suburban Commuter. . . . You've no idea how I laughed when I realized what a fool I'd been—that's a lie. I cried all day . . . I suppose you'll deny it?"

"Deny what?"

"Ah, why do I even ask," Daisy sighed, pressing her cheek against the icy pane, "when I know he will only lie by omission? . . . You know, oddly enough I think I will miss this garden the most. I always seem to miss most what I don't understand."

"Except that that particular window happens to look out on the street."

"And there was a time," Daisy said, wheeling around, "when that *particular* comment would have snowed me. No longer."

"Do facts still mean nothing to you, then?"

"Which facts? The fact that you tried to wreck my entire vision of life? The fact that you tried to crucify me over poor Seymour when all the while you—oh, it's too horrible to contemplate."

"I didn't try to crucify you. Daisy, listen to me—"

"You even almost succeeded."

"Daisy, please, you've got to—"

"And kindly stop shaking me. I happen to be a human being with wants and needs of my own, not a malted."

"Daisy, for the love of god! Will you quit horsing around and listen to me—?"

Had he really been shaking her? A pair of hands were gripping her shoulders, wrenching the material of her thin blue blouse. The hands of some hysterical maniac. His own.

"All right," George said. "So what you suspect is true. What of it? It's nothing you couldn't have figured out right in the beginning if you'd wanted to."

"Spoken like a true gatekeeper. I congratulate you."

"Besides which," George continued, flinching a little, "it happens to be totally irrelevant to the issue at hand because—"

A swooning sound interrupted him.

"—because, and get this through your head, little Miss Muffet, gatekeeper or not, I'm the only one left in this town who still gives a damn what happens to you. In fact I'm the only one left who'll ever tell you about anything."

"Oh, my former dearest love," Daisy said, "the tragedy is that you couldn't even tell me the right time any longer, don't you see that? . . . What time *is* it, by the way?"

He looked at his watch. "About four."

"Are you sure?" she said, shivering slightly. "I'd better be getting on. It feels later."

"Daisy, listen to me, you can't afford to be a child any longer. Can't you get it through your head that it will never be safe for you to go on in a town like this?"

"Safe!"

"Yes, *safe* . . . and don't look at me like that."

"Oh, how I scorn you!" Daisy cried. "Oh, how I scorn you and your miserable thin-lipped adultress! Oh, how it *hurts* me to scorn you! Now you listen to me, George Auerbach. I came here to embrace the world. I embraced you by mistake. I acknowledge the error. *Mea culpa.* But now I assure you, I shall embrace the world—or die in the attempt!"

She whipped out her coat, and as George ducked, flung it around her. A few beaded tears glittered on her cheek.

"In other words," George said, closing his eyes, "—you will now characteristically refuse to believe anything I ever tell you again. Right?"

Silence.

"Even if I—said I loved you?"

Impassioned silence.

"And if I swore," George added, squeezing his eyes tighter, "that a little bird shat on Stella Brooks and she now lies mortally ill?"

"Very funny."

He nodded delicately. "Yes. Well, good-bye, Daisy."

"Good-bye, George."

The chill of her departure swept past him and then the ridiculous uneven clatter of those high heels on the wooden stairs. He stood still, involuntarily glancing at the window through which there had never, no *never!* been a view of the garden. Well, it served a man right for meddling, for attempting to reason where reason was strangled at birth. The shade from the window chose that moment to come bouncing down to the floor and he kicked it aside. Ah, yes, there she was, stopping at the end of the walk. She had opened her thin young arms wide with her coat flared out behind her, and lifted her face to the dying sunlight which suddenly loomed over a treetop to consume her with its pink radiance. Exalté, as usual. Undoubtedly she supposed herself a little queen at this moment, or a phoenix rearisen from her own hot ashes? Well, she was mistaken. She was only a pretty little creature with pretty plumage. A tiny mass of nerve and bone caught in a very brief light. A hummingbird, maybe, pulsing on the wing . . . ?

"*Daisy!*" George cried.

But she had already picked up her suitcase and flitted on, listing to one side as usual, until the trees had dappled her completely.